Stabbing Along the Straightaway

a Thomas Ballard mystery

D.G. Stern

NEPTUNE PRESS

NEPTUNE PRESS

WWW.NEPTUNEPRESS.ORG

Publisher's Cataloging-In-Publication Data

Stern, D. G.
Stabbing along the straightaway / D.G. Stern.
Orlando, Florida : Neptune Press, 2017
A Thomas Ballard mystery
Identifiers: ISBN 978-0-9906103-5-9
1. LCSH: Automobile racing drivers--Fiction.
2. Murder--Fiction.
3. LCGFT: Detective and mystery fiction.
LCC PS3619.T477 S73 2017
DDC 813/.6--dc23

There are only three sports: bullfighting, motor racing, and mountaineering; all the rest are merely games.

— *Ernest Hemingway*—

CHAPTER ONE

Auto racing is a dangerous sport. Everyone knows that. Sometimes people are even killed-usually drivers, but there have been some horrific accidents when unwary spectators have been fatally injured. As an aside, I did hear of a driver who was crushed to death while unloading his car transporter, but that is the exception.

A driver is keenly aware of the potential of death every time he or she gets into car. It's a risk assumed, but one to be painstakingly avoided by countless hours of vehicle preparation, driver safety equipment and common sense.

So the death of driver Charles William Tyler III wasn't totally unexpected, except that he was stabbed in the back-in bed-in his motor home-at the Citrus Grove Raceway. Chip, as he insisted everyone call him, and there was some question whether he was a *chip off the old block* or always *had a chip on his shoulder*, was an up and coming competitor. Well, that isn't quite accurate because Chip never came *up*. He was the son of a very wealthy *sportsman*, Charles William Tyler, Jr., who like his offspring, never really worked a day in his life.

In his father's youth, being a *sportsman* meant you had no visible means of support, hung out at all the best places, were seen with all the best sort of people and basically contributed nothing to the world.

Chip didn't stray far from the family *business* by becoming a race car driver inasmuch as his dad bought him the coolest, fastest and most expensive cars available, many of which he wrecked. Chip also had the habit of wrecking homes as well by sleeping with the wives and girl friends of other drivers, crew members, track officials, ticket takers-actually anyone. So I guess it should not come as a complete surprise that a knife found its way into Chip's back. But who would do such a dastardly deed? The list is long.

Lest I get too far ahead, let me introduce myself. My name is Thomas Ballard, the first, and only to the best of my knowledge. My friends call me Thomas and so do my enemies, of whom I don't think I have too many. I am a free lance journalist and I cover motor sports, a/k/a car racing. I have always wanted to be a writer. I don't know why. My dad was a plumber. I am not knocking plumbers. Dad worked hard and took great care of my mom and me. I even got to go to college.

I grew up in Orlando. I am a native Floridian, quite a rarity these days. Unlike most families, both my parents loved car racing-NASCAR racing, dirt track racing, endurance racing, go-kart racing and even drag racing. As a kid we would go to New Symrna Speedway for a day of late model modified racing and then drive across the state to Bradenton to watch the evening program of funny cars.

If you think all this overdose of cars would turn me into a motor head, you are right. I thought I wanted to be a driver, but I never had the opportunity-like money or talent. You should have both, but you need at least one. So I thought about being a mechanic and maybe a crew chief, but I wasn't all that handy. I guess dad's *fix-it* genes didn't pass down to me. So I decided to write about cars and racing. I certainly knew enough about the sport and the people in the race game. I was an outgoing kid and became an outgoing adult so I had no problem getting folks to talk to me. After four years as a Gator at the University of Florida, I had become a pretty damn good journalist.

That was the good news. The bad news was finding someone who wanted to pay me for writing about cars. There are the standard monthly car magazines which are filled with reviews of cars only a few of us even dream of, let alone own, surrounded by full page ads for things which have little or no application to the real world of car junkies. I wanted to write about racing. I wanted my readers to appreciate Bubba, Tiny and Fuzzy who raced on dirt tracks or The Rattler, The Shark or The Rocket who raced down a quarter mile at crazy speeds. I even wanted my readers to follow the exploits of Luigi, Hans and Carlos as they raced open wheel formula cars all over the world. And I wanted it in real time, not once a month in a side column entitled *RACING NEWS*. I wanted everything.

Daily newspapers might give a few inches to car racing stories on a regular basis, but any real impact articles had to have special reader interest. This translated into the week before Daytona 500 the papers are filled with articles about almost everything NASCAR, except in the North, East and West, away from stock car racing's roots. NHRA is big in California, Formula 1 in the East and dirt track in the heartland. What's a writer to do?

The answer: write about every facet of the sport and sell the articles into the specific market that caters to that facet. Easier said than done. Not the writing part, but the selling part and newspapers are very cheap when it comes to compensating its writers-and slow payers.

News today is far different from even ten years ago. I never imaged selling stories to companies who syndicate my work for social media. Because of the thirst for instant news, I am suddenly in demand. It's called content. There are apps for everything, including car racing. If you are a vintage sports car fan, you download the vintage sports car app and read about what happened at Lime Rock, Road America or Monterey. The same goes for Formula 1, Indy cars, NASCAR, NHRA and even certain outlaw racing groups. I am in car heaven. I will sometimes visit five venues in a single weekend and post the articles as I travel between races.

Real time, the reason I am at The Raceway at Citrus Grove, the site of the third annual Sunshine Vintage Car and Country Music Festival, along with about 20,000 like minded spectators-and Chip Tyler.

CHAPTER TWO

Race tracks tend to fall into several categories: the old, smelly, noisy and dirty tracks where racing is about fun and friendship; the super venues where the super rich rub elbows with-the super rich, everyone else being relegated to the cheap seats so the track looks full on TV; and the multi-purpose locations where the track revenue is augmented by flea markets, concerts and even Boy Scout camp outs.

Citrus Grove is the latter, although in defense of its management, who are race car guys themselves, the track was well designed for both drivers and spectators. Since it was built only four years ago, it has excellent amenities (bathrooms) and lots of concession stands serving good food at fair prices-a rarity at entertainment venues. It is also easily accessible by most modes of transportation being situated in beautiful Central Florida, about halfway between the iconic bastions of Sebring to the south and west and Daytona to the north and east. We are the home of Mickey, Harry, two professional sports stadiums, an arena, two performing arts centers, the largest university in the United States, great shopping and nightly drive-by shootings.

The track itself is located in a section of town called Foggy Creek or Foggy Swamp depending on who you are talking to, which may explain why it isn't a hot spring of housing developments. Since it is a stone's throw from the Orlando International Airport, noise is not an issue, and parking, buses and trains abound. Disney World and Universal are less than a half hour away.

I didn't get to the track until almost midnight on Friday since I was covering an event at Volusia Speedway Park in Barberville, Florida, about an hour from Citrus Grove. Volusia is a ½ mile semi banked clay oval, which means fun, excitement and occasional contact-all in the name of sport. If something goes wrong with your race car, before the hood is off at least a dozen folks have gathered around offering advice and parts. The beer is cold and the burgers are delicious.

Housing is never a problem. I am like a turtle. I carry my house with me where ever I go. Actually, I tow my house-a beautifully restored, thanks Dad, 1955 Airstream Flying Cloud. She's gorgeous, inside and out, and practical, especially if I get to the track on the late side.

Usually when I arrive at the track at this hour, especially on the day before qualifying, except for the occasional crew pulling an *all nighter* to replace a blown engine, the place is as quiet as a mouse. Not tonight. The concert, featuring C and W new comer and teenage heart throb, Dalton Goodrich, not related to the tire company, is just letting out and traffic is nuts. Since I assume a fair amount of beer has been consumed by the departing audience, I want to be as far away as possible. Armed with my media credentials, charm and a $20 bill, I get into the RV parking area closest to the press entrance. It becomes obvious that many of the revelers are planning on staying at the track for the night and for Saturday's events, whether music or machine. I am going to be in for a rowdy night.

I start the generator in my home away from home, turn on the most obscure light I can find, open the ice box, not the refrigerator, remove a cold Pabst Blue Ribbon and say to myself, *self, it might be a good time to write and post the results of the late model races and wait for the noise to ease up a bit.* It only took one beer for three things to happen: finish my article, the ruckus to fade away and a knock on my door.

If I was pleased by the work I had accomplished, I was like totally surprised that someone is summonsing me at this hour. Then it occurs to me that it was probably one of the concert goers wanting to ask directions, use my bathroom or borrow a cup of sugar. I am very, very wrong-it is the chief steward of the race, William Clifford.

"Bill, come on in," I say opening the door to my trailer. "Hanging out with the kids at the concert? Want a beer?"

"Thanks Thomas. Yeh, I'll have a beer. Sorry to bother you this late, but I saw you come in a few minutes ago and thought you might still be up."

"No problem." I hand an obviously upset friend an *ice cold* can of PBR. "What's up?"

"I have a problem that I hope you can help me with."

"I'll try." What else can you say at midnight when you have no idea what someone is talking about?

"It's Chip Tyler."

"No surprise there, Bill. The kid is a jerk."

"He is causing quite a stir with the other drivers."

"Racing or raunchiness?" You can tell that there is not a lot of loss love between yours truly and Mr. Tyler III.

"He is going to cause an accident and someone or some very expensive machinery is going to be hurt. Can you talk some sense into him, Thomas? I think he respects you."

It is important for readers to understand that different races have different rules, written and unwritten. The code of conduct on the oval track I visited tonight is far different from the code of conduct at a vintage car race. First and foremost, oval racing has a little bumping during the race built into it. Cars are easily and often repaired. Oval track racing is also a learning platform for younger and more aggressive drivers trying to get a ride in a bigger arena of auto racing, along with sponsorship. Since I provide younger racers with media exposure, I am always welcome. I am never critical unless someone is acting like a total idiot.

Vintage racing is at the other end of the spectrum. The drivers are either older race car drivers, who are no longer actively engaged in real competition or simply older drivers who now have the money and time to race vintage cars. Whereas racing on an oval track is 100%, vintage racing is supposed to be 90%. In oval track racing the drivers are the show. In vintage car racing, the cars are the show. Many vintage cars are rare, beautifully restored and worth a fortune. Drivers are to behave like gentlemen and ladies both on and off the track.

Demographically, oval track racing and vintage racing present an interesting juxtaposition for fans and sponsors. Usually when the racing for the day has ended, drivers and crews join in companionship featuring food and beverage-burgers and beer versus buffet and Bordeaux. Neither is better than the other from my point of view, simply different. The choice of music usually reflects the age difference: Adam Lambert versus Tony Bennett, although Country and Western seems to transcend all ages, especially here in the South.

Enter our problem: Chip Tyler, who is neither older nor a gentleman. He is simply rich and drives a car about which he cares little and probably couldn't fix if he was stranded on a mountain road surrounded by howling wolves. So why is he racing with the vintage folks? The oval boys and girls, with whom he is closer in age, would probably run him off the track. And he wouldn't dare try to make a move on one of their *women*. He probably lacks the skill to drive that close and that fast with other really good drivers.

The vintage crowd is simply too polite to tell him to get lost and take his toys somewhere else-which is nowhere else. So Chip shows up with his British Racing Green 1951 Jaguar, replacing his red 1956 Alfa Romero, which he trashed during a practice session at Palm Beach International Raceway with virtually no one else on the track. The problem was not mechanical; it was Chip being-Chip.

"Thomas, he is driving way over his head and spends as much time off the track as on." Bill awakes me from my aside.

"Black flag him and give him the heave ho," I reply.

"Not that simple."

"Why not? Everyone knows the rules. I'm not even a driver and I know the rules. If you drive recklessly . . . You are suspended for the event and put on probation. If you do it again during probation, you are suspended. End of statement." I am obviously missing something. Something important enough to have the Chief Steward in a swivet.

"There's a rub, which is why I want you to talk to him."

"Okay, I'll bite. What's the rub and when do you want me to talk to him?"

"It's too late tonight." Bill is so uptight he is about to crush the beer can, which he has drained inordinately fast-even for a chief steward.

"Chip's father is one of the owners of the track. Although a silent partner, he owns the majority interest in the facility. It's a perfect venue for us. We are able to get cars and drivers from all over the world because of the location. We . . . I am afraid that if we kick out Chip, it may lead to very unpleasant results."

Ah, the cat is out of the bag. Not only did Daddy buy spoiled rich kid a race car or two, but the whole damn track, as well.

"What time is Chip's first practice session tomorrow morning, Bill?"

Unfolding a piece of paper and donning his reading glasses, Bill replies, "10 o'clock."

"Since Chip has a fulltime mechanic servicing his car, I assume he won't make an appearance until about twenty minutes before the session. I'll go over to his trailer at 8 with a cup of coffee, but I want your assurances that if I can't talk any good sense into the kid, you are going to give him the boot next time he does something dangerous. There are too many good people and great machines out there to let this over indulged jerk put them at risk. Deal?"

"Do I have a choice?"

"Of course you always have a choice, Bill. You can throw him out before I talk to him." I break into one of my Hollywood smiles.

"Thanks, Thomas. You are truly a good part of the sport."

"Bill?"

"Yes."

"You forgot to mention my charm and good looks."

"Thomas, you need a cold shower," Bill says as he grabs my hand in sincere friendship. "Thanks."

CHAPTER THREE

If you have visited as many race tracks as I have, you really learn to appreciate a shower with hot water which is also open all night. I pull out a clean towel, some equally clean (I hope) shorts, my shower shoes, flash light and toiletry kit (which I call a Dopp kit, named after Charles Doppelt who designed the popular bag). As I reach for the door handle, I hear another knock. It's 12:30 in the morning and I have to tell a rich brat to mind his manners early tomorrow morning.

Rather than ask who could possibly be bothering me at this hour, I open the door and there stands a circa 17-year-old girl, wearing the skimpiest shorts and halter top on the face of the earth and a tall, rather gawky looking, also 17ish, boy.

"Can you help us mister? We're lost," the femme fatale asks.

"And where are you trying to go?" I try not to sound really peeved, which I am.

"We were supposed to meet our friends after the concert, but they ditched us. Now we need to get to Paddock C to find our car." The young man sounds sober, but more than a little nervous. They were probably supposed to be home a couple of hours ago and realize that they are in deep doo doo with the parents.

I grab my shower stuff and step outside where the couple is holding hands. "If you turn around and look down the line of trailers, you will see a white two story building."

"Yeh, I see it," the young man almost screams.

"When you get to the building take a right turn and walk toward an opening that looks like a tunnel, which it is. Paddock C is on the other side of the tunnel. Do you remember where you parked your car? It's a pretty big area."

"Yeh, next to our friend's car," the young girl cheerfully adds. The vocabulary of these two is somewhat limited.

"You mean the friends who ditched you?" I ask.

The dynamic duo stare down at their respective feet, slowly give me eye contact and nod.

"Do you have a remote door opener for your car?"

"Yeh . . . Sure," the young man responds. "Why?"

"Here's a little trick I learned a long time ago. When you get to where you think your car is, click the remote and look around. If you see car lights flashing, bingo, you have found your car. Repeat as necessary."

"Wow, mister, you're really smart. Thanks." The couple walk off hand in hand toward what I hope is a safe journey home.

And I head to the showers-at last.

Nothing, well almost nothing, is better than a steaming hot shower, especially when you know you can now crawl under some clean, more or less, sheets and get seven uninterrupted hours of sleep. At least I can hope they will be uninterrupted, but at this juncture, I am not sure.

Morning comes entirely too early, even though my trustee gold plated imitation Rolex says 7:20, the sounds of generators, crews exchanging morning greetings and even the grumble of a race engine are starting to invade my space. No wait! Race car engines can't be started until 8 o'clock. It's the grumble of my stomach that I hear. Splash some water on my face; brush my teeth, put on a slightly wrinkled pair of jeans, comfortable sneakers and a tee shirt that says *MY OTHER CAR IS A FERRARI*. I know it's tacky, but it's clean and one can always find a Ferrari or two at a vintage car event.

It's only about 200 feet to the nearest concession stand, where a line is already forming. The smell of coffee fills my nostrils, like ambrosia. Okay, no more idiotic similes.

"I would like one breakfast special and two cups of black coffee," I tell the nice lady at the order window. I know she is nice because she smiles at me when I pay her. First things first-eat and then visit Chip Tyler.

The breakfast special consists of two eggs, hash browns, a generous slice of ham and the mandatory glass of orange juice, all for under $6. Can't be beat, even at my favorite local diner, *Pete's*, which does have the best pancakes anywhere.

Fortified, I trek across Paddock A towards a long line of RV's, all glistening in the morning dew. I have never been in the Tyler-mobile before so I am winging it. *Ah ha*, I say to myself as I spot a shiny green classic Jaguar being rolled out of a trailer attached to a hotel on wheels. Chip's version of roughing it at the track is an almost 40 foot maroon and silver Pierce coach, with sliders and awnings and a big screen TV mounted on the outside of the RV. It is bigger than the homes of many people I know.

I finish my remaining coffee and like the Greek bearing a gift, approach Chip's mansion with an offering, a still hot cup of java. The front door is slightly ajar so I assume that the occupant or occupants are stirring inside. Suddenly the door opens and a dapper, gray haired gent wearing black slacks and a white shirt exits.

"Morning." I try to sound cheerful. "Is Chip about?"

"Don't actually know." The man's accent was definitely old school British. "Haven't seen him this morning. Just popped in to get the log book for the Jag. Need to get it through tech again after the car had several off course excursions yesterday. Suspect he's still in his bedroom. Come on in and go all the way to the back of the coach. If he is not up, you can do us all a favor and get him moving. We have a practice session at 10. Cheers."

The inside of the RV is spectacular, if you like that sort of thing. I prefer the wood and earthy tones of my Airstream. Every counter surface is marble. Every appliance is stainless steel. The floor is bamboo laminate. The walls are covered with faux leather and the sitting surfaces with real leather.

At the end of the endless hallway, I spy what is likely the master bedroom, with the door slightly opened. Chip is probably awake and preparing to wreck havoc upon the vintage car world. I tap discreetly, lest I inadvertently find young Tyler in an embarrassing situation. Little did I know. I knock a bit louder and the door swings open.

"Oh shit!" I think they can hear my voice in Paddock C. Lying peacefully in his bed is Charles William Tyler III, with a very large knife protruding from his back. The pool of congealing blood tells me that he's been dead for a while, but not too long. Three things immediately enter my mind: Did I contaminate the murder scene? Who should I call? And how am I going to contain this mess with tens of thousands of people in attendance?

As to the first question, I simply don't touch anything else, make a note of what I have already touched and leave the RV, but not the vicinity. As to questions numbered two and three, the answer is simple, more or less. Growing up only about ten miles from the raceway has certain advantages, not the least of which is the Sheriff of Orange County is a high school buddy of mine and someone I respect for his competence and discretion.

Orlando is located in Orange County along with a couple of other towns. However, a large part of Orange County is unincorporated being former groves and cattle land. As a consequence the city of Orlando has a mayor and Orange County has a mayor. Orlando has a police force (OPD) and the county has a police force (Sheriff's office). The jurisdictional lines are a bit blurred, but for some reason it actually works.

In as much as it is Saturday and I think even the Sheriff gets a day off, I dial Josh McCarthy's cell phone.

"Josh, it's Thomas Ballard. There's a problem at the track." I pause. "Yes, a very serious problem and one which cannot wait."

Since the Sheriff and I have been friends for over thirty years, I think he can tell that this is not a prank call.

"Charles Tyler's kid, Chip, is dead with a very large knife in his back in the bedroom of his RV. I discovered the body or at least I think I discovered it. No telling if someone other than the killer knows."

There is a long pause on the Sheriff's side of the call and then he gives me instructions to secure the scene as subtly as possible, tell no one what has happened and await his arrival.

"Josh, there are at least 20,000 people here already and race cars are preparing to qualify for tomorrow's races. The concert begins at noon and the crowd is expected to double. Can you try and keep sirens and lights to a minimum. No point in creating a panic, especially since there are probably tons of suspects around." Again I pause.

"No he wasn't the most popular kid on the block, which will make it harder to narrow the field of potential killers to a couple of score." Once again I await instructions.

"Yes, I always carry it with me. Okay. See you in a few."

One would think I'd be in journalist heaven by finding the corpse of an important person. Well, a rich person. There's a drawback with being close to the Sheriff who appreciates my deductive reasoning and general sleuthing skill. He made me a special deputy many years ago. So I have been instructed to put on my badge, which I carry to get out of an occasional speeding ticket, and keep a lid on things until the cavalry arrives. No news scoop.

CHAPTER FOUR

I decide that I need the extra coffee I brought over more than the intended recipient and am very grateful for its remaining warmth. I am suddenly feeling cold. The rather traditional ringtone of my cell focuses me on the here and now.

I look at the caller ID-*Bill Clifford*.

"Good morning, Bill."

"Thomas, I just dropped by your trailer and hoped you were on your way to talk some sense into Chip Tyler." He sounds frantic.

Oh boy, how do I handle this? I think I had better come clean-well at least a little bit.

"Bill, all I can say is that Chip won't be racing this weekend. So you can take a deep breath and do all the things a chief steward does."

"That's really good news." I can hear Bill sigh. "Is everything alright?"

"Not really. When I got to Chip's trailer I found him in a very bad way. I called the EMT's."

"Couldn't the track medical service handle it?"

"I don't think so. It appears serious and I also don't want them tied up with Chip so that the race schedule is delayed."

"Good thinking. Thomas, you are a life saver."

How ironic.

I am now facing several pressing issues-spin control being foremost, followed by securing the RV, getting my law enforcement credentials, getting my media credentials and going to the men's room. Two cups of coffee would normally win out. It would be so much easier to use the bathroom in the RV, but if Chip had a late night visitor, based on the blood around the body, the bad guy or girl may have washed up. I guess I will have to wait until my backup arrives. I decide that the Sheriff thing is less likely to get people to talk to me than my persona of being a reporter. Josh is a great interrogator, but I think that there is a natural aversion to being candid when talking to a cop. I hope he agrees.

I settle in for guard duty by leaning against the door, folding my arms across my chest and appearing tough. My first customer shows up about two minutes later. It's the dapper fellow who was taking Chip's car to tech inspection.

"Any luck waking up sleeping beauty. I don't want to miss a qualifying session and God knows his nibs really needs some track time."

"Sorry to tell you this, but your employer won't be driving this weekend." I am trying to sound nonchalant.

"So they actually gave him the heave ho. I'm not surprised. He simply does not have either the temperament or discipline to drive in competition. As a matter of fact, he doesn't have the temperament to drive . . . Period. Guess I'll load up the Jag and get myself some breakfast. I presume Mr. Tyler will make some sort of scene. Probably call his pater, who I understand is an owner of the track and try to make everyone's collective lives miserable." With a shake of his head he turns walks toward the beautiful green car, perfectly clueless. Yes!

Within what seems like an hour, but is only about five minutes, Sheriff McCarthy arrives, driving his wife's mini-van. He is wearing jeans, sneakers and a Dale Earnhardt, Jr. number 88 tee shirt. The perfect cover for a cop at a car race-country festival.

"Josh. I'll be right back," I announce as he alights from the vehicle.

"What's up, Thomas?"

"Later," I reply as I virtually run to the nearest bathroom. I hear him laughing uncontrollably. That's being mean spirited, but I don't care at this point.

"Glad you survived," Josh quips upon my return.

"How in hell did I know I was going to have to babysit a corpse after two cups of coffee?"

"Fill me in." Josh is all professional.

"I made a couple of executive decisions while I was waiting for you."

Josh gives me his one eye brow raised stare.

"Since the reason I went to visit the deceased this morning was because of his unacceptable conduct on the race track, I had to notify the chief steward that Chip would not be racing this weekend. I told him in very vague terms that Chip was not well and that I had called the EMT's. Initially he seemed concerned that I didn't reach out to the track medics, but I assured him that it would be less disruptive if it was handled from the outside. He seemed okay with that."

"Good cover story."

Suddenly the Chief's cell phone starts to play Beethoven's 5th Symphony. He answers.

"We are about half way down the long line of car transports, before you reach the two story white building. No siren or lights. You'll see me."

I walk to the front of the RV and peer down the road. A bright red rescue truck, which is just like the rescue vehicles used by the raceway, slowly approaches, followed by an unmarked dark blue Sheriff's Department Ford Explorer.

Josh raises his hand and points toward a space next to the RV's door. He points to the driver of the Explorer and then points to an open parking area about twenty feet further away. He is keeping this low profile.

"I want to tell you the other executive decision I made. I have decided to go undercover as a journalist. I think it is more effective than being a cop for getting people to speak openly."

The Sheriff nodded. "Good idea." Josh can be a man of few words.

Three deputy sheriffs approach from the Explorer and begin to dust sections of the RV, primarily the door to the living area. The deputies work quickly, but inconspicuously. Since race cars are preparing for qualifying, no one seems to give the police presence a second thought.

"Josh, there is one other person who is aware that the victim won't be racing . . . His mechanic . . . A Brit who simply went about his business and loaded Chip's car onto the transporter. Said he was going to get some breakfast and await his employer's next assignment. He assumes Chip was booted out of the race for poor driving and he didn't seem a bit surprised."

"Good."

"Outside all done, Sheriff," a deputy announces, "Including the area immediately around the RV. Lots of good finger prints, but no foot prints, fluids or anything else of any use."

"I have an idea Josh," I suggest.

"Okay."

"Why not have one of your guys drive the entire rig to the facility on the Trail and then you can do a full forensic evaluation without worrying about curiosity seekers, and it will allow me to ask questions without raising any suspicion that there was foul play. Maybe the EMT's can go in and say *he's dead* but otherwise leave him in the bed for you guys to check everything with a fine tooth comb. I've got to believe there is something in the RV that will provide clues."

"Another good idea," the loquacious Sheriff replies. He turns to one of the officers and says, "Williams, can you drive this rig to headquarters impound?"

"Sure, Sheriff."

"Dust the area around the driver's seat, steering wheel, shift knob, inside door handle and then I want you to carefully get going."

"Another suggestion?" I hope I am not being a pain.

"Go."

"I think you should make sure that the transporter is hitched up so that people think Chip is leaving for the weekend. Also you may get prints from the Jaguar and maybe there's a large knife missing from the tool box. You know."

"Want my job?"

"Nope." I can be as terse of Sheriff McCarthy

"Valdez, check that the race car is secured inside the trailer and that the trailer is secure to the RV."

"Yes, sir."

"Corporal?" The Sheriff's attention is directed to the remaining deputy.

"Yes, Sir," the tall, blond, female officer answers. She is very attractive in an, *if you cross me I will rip your head off* kind of way.

"When Valdez is through, take him and follow Williams back to impound. I want a full forensic on the RV, the trailer and the victim. You're in charge. Anyone questions your authority or gives you a hard time because it's Saturday, have them call me. I'll be here with special deputy Ballard." Now that got a surprise reaction.

"Want a cup of coffee?" I ask Josh as Chip's rig pulls away, followed at a discreet distance by the unmarked Explorer and the emergency vehicle which never did anything except tell the Chief that Chip was indeed dead, which I already knew.

CHAPTER FIVE

"Hey wait!" A voice screams. It's Tyler's Brit mechanic who has not only lost his race car, but his employer as well.

I quickly step in front of his mad dash after the RV. "Take a deep breath and I'll explain everything."

"You're the chap who was supposed to wake up Mr. Tyler. What in bloody hell is going on?"

"Josh . . . " I intentional do not address him in his official capacity. "This gentleman works for Chip Tyler." I intentionally do not use the past tense. Turning to the obviously confused mechanic, I say, "I'm sorry, I don't even know your name."

"Hooker . . . L. Frederick Hooker, but everyone calls me Freddy, which is a lot better than being called *hooker*.

I like this guy. He has a typical Limey sense of humor despite his driver being killed, which he is about to find out.

"Another executive decision coming up." I look at Chief McCarthy.

"I suppose," he replies.

"Freddy, would join us in a coffee? There is a lot I want to tell you. I'm being rude again. My name is Thomas Ballard and this is a colleague of mine Josh McCarthy."

"You are the car racing reporter fellow, right?"

"Guilty as charged." Josh lets out a low groan at my attempt to be cleaver.

"How do you do gents?" Freddy shakes our hands. His grip is firm.

"I've got another idea."

"Lord help us," the Sheriff says.

"Have I ever steered you wrong? No, wait don't answer. Since college?"

"I haven't kept count. I am afraid to think about it." Freddy is glancing back and forth between Josh and me.

"You blokes go way back, don't you?"

"Probably too far back." Is that a smile I see upon the face of our esteemed representative of law enforcement?

"Excuse me one second. I need to call Bill Clifford," I announce.

"Why?" Josh asks.

"Another executive decision." I start to dial.

"Bill, Thomas Ballard, I need a favor."

"Thomas, you don't need to ask, just tell me what you want. I am forever grateful for your help."

"A friend of mine decided to come down to the track for the day and he needs press credentials. Since I haven't even picked mine up, I thought I would kill two birds so to speak and get a pass for him. Doable?" Did I really say *kill two birds*?

"No problem. What's his name and does he have a picture ID? They're a little picky about ID's now days," the overworked chief steward says.

"His name is Josh McCarthy and he has a picture ID."

The Chief nods as he begins to figure out where I am going with this.

"I'll call it in now. Give them about fifteen minutes to print up the credentials. Do you need banquet tickets for tonight?"

"Thanks Bill. Three tickets would be great."

"Who's the third? I need to add it to the list."

"Freddy Hooker. Chip Tyler's mechanic."

Josh is about to fall over in hysterics. He has figured out exactly how we are going to gather information without arousing suspicion.

"Welcome to the fourth estate, cub reporter McCarthy."

"Before I knuckle your head, let me pay you a compliment. Albeit a very little compliment . . . Well done. Let's get that coffee. Ready, Freddy?" Help us all if the Sheriff of Orange County is going to start being funny.

Any hope of further conversation is lost immediately after the announcer broadcasts: *Group 6 report to the false grid.* About 15,000 horsepower is suddenly unleashed as Corvettes, Mustangs, Camaros and Cobras line up for their qualifying session.

CHAPTER SIX

Needless to say our initial interviewee is Freddy and depending on how it goes, he may be our first assistant. He can talk to people who might be reticent talking to even a couple of car racing reporters. They would completely clam up to a cop.

"Freddie, how do you like your coffee?" Josh asks.

"Just hot water, please."

"Thomas?"

"Black, please."

"Grab a picnic table at the back of the tent," Sheriff McCarthy suggests, in his, *this is really an order* type voice.

Freddie and I need no additional coaxing.

We both say a few perfunctory *hellos* to other patrons and find a table at the far corner of the concession area. Josh joins us bearing three steaming cups. He hands Freddie his water. I guess I shouldn't be surprised. Our perfectly proper Jaguar mechanic reaches into his pocket and retrieves a bag of Earl Gray tea.

Without prompting he says, "I never travel without my own tea bags. Can't stand the stuff they serve."

"May we ask you a few questions about the Chip Tyler?" I ask.

"Fire away." Freddie seems all too willing.

"I guess I have two questions: how long have you known Chip? And what do you think of him?"

"I'll be perfectly up front with you," Freddie starts, "If you are perfectly willing to be upfront with me . . . Sheriff McCarthy."

"Whoa, cat is already out of the bag," I say half to myself. Josh is stone faced.

"I have a confession to make," Freddie offers. Now that's got our attention. "I am a news junkie, mostly television since I don't have much time for nor interest in printed news with all apologies Mr. Ballard. Our shop is in Melbourne, so we are in the Orlando viewing area and Sheriff McCarthy; you are on the news a lot. Always good, I might add. So let me assure you that I am the portrait of discretion, but please tell me what the bloody hell is going on."

"Thomas found your employer dead this morning, in his RV, with a knife in his back."

"Damn." Freddie's eyes begin to moisten. "You know, I think the kid was really trying to break out of the spoiled, brat mold. He hadn't gotten there, but over the last few months, I was seeing the makings of a nice young man."

"Freddie, we need your help and we need it badly. Please give us an overview of your relationship with Chip Tyler and his father. You know what is at stake, so please don't leave anything out, even if you think it is trivial." Freddie nods at me.

"And Freddie, we want to maintain the cover of Thomas and I being reporters, so please call me Josh and him Thomas."

"Understood. Let me begin about two years ago. I had call from a friend of mine in Palm Beach, who runs a shop much like ours; preparing and servicing exotic and vintage race cars. He is quite good, but he lacks tact. It's his way or the highway. He is good enough that it works . . . Usually. Not so with Tyler father and son. The old man was demanding and cheap and the son was always blaming others for his abysmal driving . . . Mostly his mechanic. After Master Chip destroyed a beautiful little Alfa claiming mechanical failure, the Tylers and my friend parted ways. Parenthetically, I personal checked out the Alfa and the only problem I found was that the driver didn't know how to drive."

As our resource drinks his tea, I start to take notes. I fear a long list of people who might have wanted to do in Chip Tyler. However, his death is only a part of the puzzle. The method of death is very significant. I can imagine Tyler bad-mouthing his former mechanic, but I can't imagine it rising to the level of back stabbing. A fist fight, maybe, but a knife, at night, while the victim was in bed, in the back, is not the typical way of resolving disputes amongst members of the racing community.

"I met Mr. Tyler, father not son, when he came into our shop. I have two partners and about three or four full time members of the staff, with skills ranging from fabrication to painting to hand stitched leather. Our clients are demanding, but in the most part, reasonable, and they pay us well, but we service them well. We offer several levels of at the track services, including transporting and maintaining the vehicle during race meetings. Anyway, Mr. Tyler approached us to purchase a car for his son . . . The Jag. The price was fair, but not chump change. He didn't know that I was aware of the Alfa debacle and I decided to keep a lid on it. Why ruin a sale?"

"Freddie, what is the name of your friend in Palm Beach?" Josh's voice is barely above a whisper.

"Whistler . . . Billy Whistler. Calls his shop "Whistler's Place". It's actually in West Palm Beach. Funny, just realized that I'm a Hooker and he's a Whistler." Our speaker starts to chuckle to himself. Maybe he needs another tea. We need to move this narrative along. I sense Josh is also getting impatient, but Freddie's background may help. I hope so. It's almost noon and the concert people will be flocking to the track. Also, since the first round of qualifying is almost done, we will be competing with drivers and crew members at the food stand and we really don't want to be seen with Freddie.

"I don't want to get too far behind, so I would appreciate it if we could hurry along your views on Chip Tyler and his father," Sheriff McCarthy says.

"I understand. I am still a little shell shocked and I have been drifting. The senior Mr. Tyler purchased the car and set up an eight race support contract where I personally would maintain the car and deliver it to the track. This is only the second race under the relationship. I prepped the Jag and did some road testing. It is a great car. The first event was at a small track near Savannah. Perfect learning course, except that young Master Tyler thought he knew everything. Most of the day was spent inspecting damage caused by simply poor driving. I was about ready to cancel the balance of the contract. However several things intervened: the season had ended in Florida for a couple of months, young Tyler started to show an interest in the mechanical part of racing, he met a young lady and . . . This might be important, young Tyler demonstrated an amazing gift for water color painting, especially cars. Before you both think I've lost my marbles, young Charles, I never liked the name Chip, was both indulged and controlled by his father. The mother had died while the young man was a mere toddler and he was raised by a series of nannies for hire, who, from what he began to talk about, were not Mary Poppins."

"Please Freddie," I beg, "Tell us what is important about the painting."

"Simply said, it made him feel good about himself probably for the first time in his life. He painted several customers' cars and when they saw the works, they each bought one . . . At a rather handsome price. Young Charles had his own money and a sense of purpose. He started to listen to suggestions about a myriad of things. He actually started to work on his own car. Little things at first, like changing oil. I believe he would have done a lot more in the future." Freddie stops, again with moist eyes. "Excuse me. I finally felt like I was getting through to him."

"Who do you think wanted to kill him?" Josh can be very forthright in his questioning.

"There is the obvious. Since he had perfected the role of being a jerk over most of his life, the list is probably long, but you don't kill someone for being a jerk. His reputation for being a womanizer was mostly in his own mind, although there was a grain of truth, but again, I don't believe that the number of trysts was nearly as large as Charles would have liked others to have thought. It was his bad boy image he was cultivating. However, once Monica, that's his lady friend, came on the scene, he was a very changed young fellow. He was polite and deferential to her. As a matter of fact after he sold his first paintings, he bought her a very nice pair of diamond earrings. I remember she came into the shop with Charles' father, put her hands behind her ears and said to me *don't you think I look good in diamonds?* I was a bit taken aback, but since it didn't seem to upset Charles, I didn't care."

"Did Monica come to the shop often?" I ask

"Master Tyler was spending more time tending to his car. She would pop in from time to time. Actually come to think about it, recently she would arrive with Charles' father whenever she came around."

"Very interesting." You can almost hear the wheels turning in Josh's head.

I am not sure we aren't already too much into it. Did I just use a double negative?

"Anything else, Freddie?" The Sheriff asks.

"How was Chip acting since you two arrived at the track?" I inquire.

"At first, okay. Maybe a little nervous. But then he returned to his damn fool persona. His demeanor total regressed. He got into the car and it was as if Mr. Hyde had invaded Dr. Jekyll's body. He drove foolishly and almost wrecked the Jag, which is how we met this morning. I had to retrieve the log book so the tech inspectors could re-examine the car."

"Did he have any visitors yesterday or receive any phone calls about which you are aware?" I think there is something amiss.

Josh picks up his cell and speed dials. "Corporal . . . I want you to find the decedent's cell phone and get me information on all incoming and outgoing calls since Thursday at 9 pm. I may need more, but that's a start and I want it . . . Yup . . . Now. Also, do you have an approximate time of death?" The Sheriff listens and then says, "As soon as the initial toxicology findings come in let me know. Thanks." He pushes the end button and says, "Time of death was between around midnight and about 2 in the morning. Cause of death was internal bleeding, caused by the knife in his back, no doubt."

"Freddie, the Sheriff will get the phone records, but we need you think back on any communication he had over the last 24 hours. Did he see anyone? Did he talk to his father or to Monica? Anyone?"

"I did not overhear any conversation, but upon reflection, Charles' demeanor radically changed Friday morning between the time I left to get the car initially inspected and when I returned about 30 minutes later. Master Tyler was supposed to change into his driver's suit so we could be ready for the first practice session. When I got back to the trailer, he hadn't changed. He was sullen and when I suggested he put a hop to it, he snapped at me saying something like *mind your own business*. I was curious, but chose not to say or do anything except to tell him I would be in our shop trailer whenever he required my services. We have another customer's car down here and used the company RV and trailer to transport it. I also sleep there. Wanted to give Charles privacy if he wished it."

"It's getting late and we need to get our credentials before we get the heave ho from the track. Freddie, could you discretely chat with some of your colleagues about their opinions of and feelings toward Chip Tyler. You know the situation as well as we do. Ask if anyone saw him yesterday morning and more importantly last night. Did he have a late night visitor? The place was full of concert goers."

Freddie nods.

"Josh, this is actually your bailiwick, I am just thinking like a journalist answering *who, what, where, why and when*. I think we can be pretty sure about *how*."

"Thomas, my main concern at this point is whether you are going to run against me in the next election for Orange County Sheriff. Only kidding . . . Maybe. I think that we should meet back here about 5 o'clock. I will have gotten preliminary reports from the forensic folks and hopefully Mr. Tyler's phone records. Freddie, we are asking a lot of you, but you have so far provided us more background than we could have gotten in several days of interviews. We have a lot of ground to cover and very little time within which to do it."

"I'm all in Sheriff. I liked the kid and I don't like what happened to him or how. Stabbing someone in the back is cowardly. Meet you chaps here in . . . Goodness, it's almost 1 o'clock. Cheers."

Mr. Hooker rises and rushes off.

"He will be a big help, I think." I gaze at Josh who is staring off at nothing.

"Come on. Let's get those credentials, Thomas."

CHAPTER SEVEN

In order to get to the registration building, we have to walk about a mile. I knew there was a reason why I stop to get my credentials before I enter the track. As we trek, we talk.

"We have two windows of time on which we should concentrate," Sheriff McCarthy says.

"I agree. What happened Friday morning to put young Tyler into such a bad mood and what happened Friday night to get him killed?"

"I hope his phone records will open the first window." Josh doesn't seem too sure.

"A log of whom he called and who called him will help, but let me postulate that Tyler may have made a call, but didn't get through, so he left a voice mail on the recipient's phone. That will be a problem . . . Yes?"

"In the short term, yes, but if we have calls from the decedent's phone we should be able to get a search warrant. It could be done as early as late this afternoon."

I noticed how quickly my friend is depersonalizing Chip Tyler, from the living to the dead. I guess it comes with handling as many homicides as he has during his career.

"Josh, we are assuming that your guys can find the phone."

"Shit. That's a good point. I'm going to call Corporal Nederfield. She is really thorough and I have confidence in her judgment. I'd promote her, but the union would be all over me. She does her work and minds her own business, smart as a whip and doesn't seem to have an agenda except to do her job."

The Sheriff's cell phone ring startles both of us.

"McCarthy here," he answers. "Let me put you on speaker so Special Deputy Ballard can hear this."

"Gentlemen, we are making some progress. Deputy Ballard . . . "

"It's Thomas, just plain Thomas." I interrupt.

"Thomas, your suggestion that we move everything to impound was brilliant. We have been able to go over the crime scene methodically, without worrying about contamination, rubber-neckers or . . . The press. Sorry about that."

Josh gives me a *thumbs up* and asks, "What have you got for us so far?"

"Six sets of very good prints and lots of partials. So far we have identified prints from both the deceased and his father. They both have permits to carry concealed weapon here in Florida so that was easy. Also I have identified Special Deputy . . . I mean Thomas' prints; they are here on file at the office. There is another set of prints which we found only in the driver's area of the RV. They belong to an English national, L. Frederick Hooker. His prints were matched from his immigration green card. One of the other set of prints is small leading me to think it is a woman. We have nothing on record, so I have sent the prints up the chain for comparison. The last set of prints is interesting. They are quite large and show a lot of scarring. I have also set those to Washington."

"Toxicology?"

"Not yet, Sheriff. We have a full crew on site, but we wanted to take our time with the RV before we moved the body."

"Corporal, have you found Mr. Tyler's cell phone?" I cross my fingers.

"Yes, sir. We have checked it for prints and are in the process of tracking the call log and . . . Excuse me . . . Hack into his voice mail."

Josh is smiling like a Cheshire cat.

"Well done," he says with the pride of a father. "Very well done."

"Thank you, sir. Just doing what I thought you would do."

This mutual admiration is getting a little thick.

"I have made another executive decision," I announce.

"Now what?" Josh mutters.

"Corporal, can you attend a debriefing at 5 o'clock this afternoon at the track and plan on attending a simple buffet dinner? It will give us all a chance to compare notes and everyone connected with the race will be in attendance at the feast."

"Sheriff?" She asks demurely.

"It appears it's Thomas' show and as you said, *he has been brilliant* . . . So far."

"Excuse me, but what does one wear to a race track soiree?"

Josh stares at me and shrugs.

"Please do not take this the wrong way, Corporal. But our goal is to get people to talk to us. Car racing is a bit chauvinistic, although vintage racing is less so than most venues. I suggest something casual, elegant and understated. I don't want men drooling and I don't want women to be threatened. Jeans, polo shirt, a simple gold chain and a sweater because it will get chilly. Don't wear open toe shoes. The function is going to be in a tent, but on grass and Florida ants can get very nasty. We may even have to interact with the concert crowd."

"Thomas, you should work for a fashion magazine." Sheriff McCarthy is trying to suppress a laugh.

"Thank you, Thomas. That was very helpful." I think Corporal Nederfield is looking forward to our outing. "And call me Olivia."

"Okay, let's get this show on the road!" Josh can be such a party pooper. "Call me with any updates. See you at 5 o'clock."

"Olivia, when you get to the track, just give your name to the folks at registration and we will meet you where Tyler's RV had been parked," I add. "Later."

Josh pushes the end button on his phone just as mine begins to ring. I check the caller ID. "Hi, Bill. Seems like the first qualifying session went off without a hitch." I pause. "We're headed up there right now. Yeh, we'd love a ride. Meet you in front of the medical building in two minutes. Thanks."

"I know I am somewhat demanding and impatient," Sheriff McCarthy begins.

"Somewhat?"

"Okay wise guy. What did you get from Corporal Nederfield's report?"

"I think the fact that Freddie's fingerprint were only in the driver's compartment takes him completely off our radar screen." I breathe a sigh of relief since we have taken Freddie into the inner circle.

"I agree. What about papa Tyler's prints?"

"I don't know enough about their relationship to explain or dismiss his prints in the RV. I can't see him killing the kid. He has spent a life time creating his son in his own image."

"And the smaller prints?"

"Could be his girl friend or someone else's girl friend. We forgot to ask if there were prints on the murder weapon."

"You've watched too many bad TV cop shows." I should ask Josh if there are any good cop TV shows. "Prints on weapons are either so smudged that they are of no use in identifying the killer or are wiped clean. Since Corporal Nederfield didn't mention it, I assume that to be the case." Once again Beethoven summonses the Sheriff.

"McCarthy," he announces. I wish he would look at his caller ID before he answers. "Yes. That's what I assumed. Thanks for calling back." Josh hangs up and turns to me.

"Don't tell me," I respond. "It was Olivia telling you that there were no useable prints on the knife."

"Bingo!"

"Thomas, over here," the Chief Steward shouts.

CHAPTER EIGHT

Everyone who is anyone in the car racing world has a golf cart for personal transportation to and from various track related activities, like getting gas, getting tires, getting coffee and getting seen by other people in their golf carts. If you have never heard of *The Villages*, Google it up, then you will understand the fascination with golf carts, especially here in Florida. Since time is of the essence, I am glad to indulge and get a ride to registration and back, while I subtly ask Bill some questions.

"Everything going well?" I ask.

"No major incidents, thanks to you," the Chief Steward smiles. "Couple of small off track expeditions, a Triumph broke an axle coming onto the straightaway, but the driver did a good job at steering the car to a safe area, a newly restored Group 5 Lola experienced some teething problems, mostly electrical. You know the stuff you expect. All in all, I couldn't be happier. We are on schedule and no one has yelled at me."

"Have you heard from Chip Tyler or his father?" Josh is very coy.

"No, actually. You said that Chip was not well, but I would have thought the old man would have been asking why Chip isn't racing."

"Maybe no one told him Chip has left the track," I suggest.

"Believe me; I am not upset that Mr. Tyler hasn't called."

"Bill?" Sheriff McCarthy asks in a voice that is again barely above a whisper. "Is either Chip's father or his girl friend on the banquet list for tonight?"

"I don't know, but we'll ask at registration, which is where I assume you are heading. I can add your names at the same time." The Chief Steward pats the front seat for me to join him. Josh is relegated to the back facing jump seat.

The additional four hundred pounds of weight certainly slows the cart's ascent to the registration booth, but it beats walking.

After getting our credentials, making sure that we all were all on the invitation list, including Olivia, and ascertaining that neither Monica nor Chip's father were scheduled to attend, we veritably fly down the hill to the track.

"Would you two like to join me in the tower for the next qualifying session?"

I quickly balance the need to keep up our journalism cover, with the time away from the investigation. Since we are waiting for the beautiful Corporal Nederfield to get back to us with fingerprint IDs and phone records, a twenty minute break watching the Groups 1 and 3 cars qualify could be fun and I wanted to ask Bill a few more questions.

To those not entirely familiar with vintage racing, cars are divided by class depending on age, make of car and engine size. For example open wheel cars or formula cars, which appear to be cigars with wide tires, race together because they handle differently than close wheeled cars. Sports racing cars or "specials" were originally built as race cars and are extremely fast, nimble and exotic. Production cars are those which were originally sold to customers to drive on the street. They have been modified by both hobbyists and professionals, but are required to keep their basics; engine, transmission and body design and material, but are mandated to have safety equipment; roll bar, belts, fuel cell and fire extinguisher. In all classes, the driver is required to wear a fire proof suit, glove, socks and shoes, current helmet, neck bracing system and common sense.

The race we are going to watch is to me quite often the most fun because the cars in Groups 1 and 3 are small; production based sports cars. I remember these steeds zipping around country roads like they were on rails, waiving at each other. MGs, Austin Healeys, Triumphs, Alfas, Minis (the real ones), early Porsches, Sunbeam Alpines and even a tiny Abarth fill the grid. There are 38 cars lined up for the qualifying race and when the green flag falls to start the session, it sounds like a thousand angry bees.

The cars are very competitive with one another, although each race car has idiosyncrasies. It makes for close and exciting racing. The cars are painted every color in the rainbow: the yellow and blue Sprite, the red and green Alfa, the silver Porsche, the black Triumph and the white Alpine. The only time to talk to Bill is after the last car passes the tower at the start/finish line and the first car enters the straightaway, which after about five minutes on this tight track, is almost the same time. While the cars are somewhat equal, the drivers are not, although everyone is on their best behavior and other than a flat tire on a little orange Mini, the race finishes perfectly with an MGA, a Porsche speedster and an amazingly fast red and black Fiat roadster all closing on the start/finish line within a hair's breadth.

Josh punches his fist in the air when the checker flag falls. I think he is enjoying himself and I make a note to invite him to a race when there is less pressing business.

"Quite a race," our omnipresent Chief Steward says.

"Great . . . And thanks." Sheriff McCarthy extends his hand, which Bill grabs.

"See you tonight, when I can relax." Bill seems cheerful, and I guess if the race schedule proceeds on time, with no accidents and competition as close as this last race, it's a great day.

We walk down the tower stair and stop at the bottom.

"What, oh great journalist, did you just observe?" I am not sure the purpose of Josh's question.

"I am not following you, big guy," I reply.

"Your Chief Steward has huge hands and they are heavily scarred," Josh responds.

"I follow, but it makes no sense. What's the motive?"

"Don't know. Maybe it's a domestic thing, maybe it's just that young Tyler was on the cusp of ruining the entire race by being a dangerous driver and your friend was powerless to do anything about it because daddy owns the track."

"Wow, that's something to think about." I sound a bit unsure, but it is something to think about.

"Consider this, Thomas, Mr. Clifford knocks on your trailer at midnight and basically asks you to discover Tyler's body the next morning."

"Still, there's no motive."

"Yet."

The Sheriff of Orange County has a bit of a bee in his bonnet. He speed dials. "Corporal, please check out William Clifford. He's the Chief Steward at the race track. Definitely. Thanks."

"I got it! She's going to run the unknown set of prints with his."

"Correct, Sherlock. I need a Dr. Pepper. Let's go."

CHAPTER NINE

Things are getting busy. The crowd has increased exponentially. The concert type and the car type are both absorbing the ambiance. The cacophony of sounds: the cars-the music-the people, makes ordinary conversation impossible. I think that Josh relishes a few private moments with his thoughts. I know that I do.

The concession stand has a line almost as long as a line at Disney World. Fortunately, the track designers have strategically installed beverage machines every hundred feet or so. Our deep in thought Sheriff reaches into his pocket and removes a wrinkled dollar bill. After being rejected about six times by the vending machine, we hear a clicking sound and a bottle dropping down the chute. Josh reaches into the machine and retrieves-a bottle of water.

"Thomas, what just happened?"

"You put in a buck and out came water," I reply

"Yeh, but I didn't push a selection button . . . And I don't want water. I want a Dr. Pepper." My friend is starting to whine.

"Here's the deal. I want water and I'll buy you a Dr. Pepper and then all will be right with the world." I try not to break into hysterics because I just said the same thing I would say to a petulant teenager.

"Good plan. I might even have to promote you to honorary special deputy first class." Josh reaches into the machine again and this time gets his Dr. Pepper. "I'm not going to ask you how you did that."

"Elementary, my dear Watson. I used a crisp dollar bill and gently, but firmly pushed the selection button."

"Cheers," Sheriff McCarthy says and promptly chugs the entire can of soda. It's like the old Super Bowl Coke ad with Mean Joe Greene.

"Feel better?" I snidely ask.

"Why yes," he replies, "and it's time to catch a killer."

"I'll drink to that." I only take a swallow or two before my phone rings and vibrates. "Shit!"

"Who is it?" The Sheriff asks.

"Bill Clifford," I answer. "Hi, Bill. What's up? Just don't return the call. I'll get back to you in a few minutes." I push the END button.

With one eye brow significantly higher than the other, Josh asks, "And?"

"Chip's father just called Clifford. Left a message that he wanted to know where his son was."

"I'm glad he didn't get through. I want to think about it a minute."

The minute lasts about ten seconds before Josh's phone begins to ring. "McCarthy, here," he barks into his cell. "Hold on for a second until we can get to a place where we can hear you."

We duck around the corner of building which houses cars used by the track at its driver's school.

"Okay, what do you have? I'm going to speaker phone." He mouths the words *Corporal Nederfield.*

"I have a few interesting factoids," she begins. "The other set of large prints is a perfect match for your William Clifford, a former IRS field auditor from Miami."

"Olivia, this is Thomas," I shout as another qualifying race begins. "What are you holding back?"

"How perceptive, special deputy Ballard," she purrs.

"First class. I just got a promotion for finding Dr. Pepper."

"What?"

"Don't pay the idiot journalist any mind, what else did you find?" The Orange County Sheriff can be a real wet blanket.

"Clifford left the IRS after a twenty one year, otherwise unremarkable, career. He worked primarily out of Miami. Upon retirement he joined another ex-IRS agent and two others and formed a consulting firm, providing tax and other financial advice to individuals and entities, in the then expanding field of South Florida real estate. They secured all the necessary licenses to be registered financial advisors, which is why I was able to match his prints so quickly."

"Anything problematic about Clifford's partners?" asks the Sheriff.

"Before I came to work for you, Sheriff, I was an investigator in the attorney general's office . . . Fraud division, concentrating on real estate investment trusts. After the boom went bust, we were swamped with sub-prime loan cases. Several of the groups being investigated were represented by Clifford's company, called Sunrise Investment Partners, which we all referred to as the Sunset Boys, since every deal had serious problems."

"Olivia, wasn't that simply endemic in Florida at the time?" I ask.

"True, but the deals and the players were shady from the get-go. The crash only accelerated the speed of failure," Corporal Nederfield answered.

"Anything suspicious about Clifford himself?" I am grasping for straws.

"Not really, but his clients were really suspicious. We are talking about mail, wire and bank fraud. That's only part of it. I remember a case, actually two cases, both involving golf course housing developments and both owned by the same group-Putter Development Holdings, LLC."

"Clever corporate name, but, Corporal, we seem to be running out of time, but not suspects," Josh adds.

"Bottom line is that one Charles William Tyler, Jr. was the managing member of Putter. Yes, the father of the deceased."

"Shit! Excuse me Corporal," the Sheriff stammers, "The dance floor is getting crowded and the band isn't playing."

"Josh, what do you mean by that?"

"Just being literary in your presence." Josh smiles.

At that very instant, a new group started playing at the concert.

"They're playing your tune." I return the smile.

"Gentlemen, if you don't mind, I am not done. I have not been able to get access to young Tyler's cell call log, but I have been told, it should be shortly . . . Whatever that means. I am also waiting on the smaller set of fingerprints, except that there are three sets of prints, not one." At least Olivia gave him back his name.

"Like in three different women?" I am sure I am stuttering.

"That's what it seems to indicate," she replies.

"Eliminating young Tyler, Thomas and Mr. Hooker, we've got five sets . . . Right?" The Orange County Sheriff is clearly unhappy. "I want fewer suspects, not more. Corporal, get me the ID on those prints as soon as possible . . . And the call log."

"Sheriff, as soon as I get the phone log, I will match up the numbers with the people whose prints we have. Does anyone know the last name of the girlfriend?"

"Freddy!" The Sheriff and I shout out together.

"We'll get right back to you. Good work . . . And thanks." The Sheriff glances at me after ending the call.

"I think we should split up for fifteen minutes, search for Freddy and meet back here," I suggest.

"Yup." Josh turns and starts to walk toward the concession stand and I head towards paddock A.

CHAPTER TEN

I approach a group of trailers in my search for Freddy. "Any of you guys see Freddy Hooker?" I ask to anyone within ear shot.

An older mechanic who is studying a carburetor with incredible intensity gazes up and says, "He was here about ten minutes ago. Lost his driver for the weekend and was asking if anyone needed him to lend a hand. I think he was relieved that the kid decided to pull out. I didn't figure even Freddy could put up with the father or the son. Bad business . . . Those two. I think he went to talk with some guy at RPM Racing. Big yellow trailer."

"Thanks."

"If I can't fix this damn carb, I might be looking for his help."

It seems as though our new assistant is making inquiries. I decide to finish my water so that I am not carrying around a plastic bottle that makes a crunching sound every time I move. Along with the plethora of beverage machines, are a plethora of trash cans neatly labeled *RECYCLES* and *TRASH*. After disposing the bottle, I decide to once again visit the facilities, where I meet-Freddie.

"Too much tea," he chuckles.

"Know what you mean. I was just coming to find you. Any progress?"

Freddie peers under each bathroom stall and says, "All clear. What I have discovered is that both Charles and his father are universally disliked . . . But not hated. I make the distinction so that we can fine tune the search for a motive. Dislike does not lead to murder. Also, the more I think about it, the more I conclude that the killer was someone who knew Charles."

I notice that Freddie, unlike either Josh or Olivia, still refers to young Tyler by his name, rather than depersonalizing him.

"I was tracking you down to ask a specific question," I begin. "Do you know the last name of Chip's, I mean Charles', girlfriend Monica?"

"Let me think a moment." Freddie actually strokes his chin. "Strange. As a matter of fact I don't know her surname. I was introduced to her as Monica. I seldom addressed her directly, but when I did, I remember saying *Miss Monica*. Sorry I can't be of more help."

"It's only important to speed up the identification process of the fingerprints we found."

"Keep me posted. See you at 5 o'clock. Cheers." Freddie turns and goes-to where ever he is going.

Since I have the information or lack thereof for which I went on this journey, I hustle back to meet Josh. My phone vibrates before I hear the ring tone. "Yes, Sheriff McCarthy," I answer. "Be right there."

Cars are gridding for the next session and I bob and weave around the sleek machines, hoping I won't be run down by an over-stimulated driver.

Josh is leaning against the wall of the driver's school building with his cap pulled over his eyes. Without glancing up he says, "I struck out. No one has seen Mr. Hooker."

"But I have." I resist saying *nah nah*. "He was never introduced to Monica using her last name. But he did glean that neither father nor son Tyler were well thought of amongst those with whom he spoke, but nothing close to the level of animus usually associated with murder. He is going to continue his investigation."

"Let's hope Corporal Nederfield comes up with something quickly. I want you to be able to get back to Clifford with a touch more background. I need to sit down at a table and put everything down on paper."

"Let's go back to my trailer. It's quiet."

"Good idea. Lead on, Macduff." The Sheriff makes a sweeping gesture with his arm.

"Actually, it's *Lay on, Macduff, and damned be him who first cries 'Hold! enough!'*

"I hate a *know it all*."

I am saved from making a reply by Beethoven.

"McCarthy," Josh literally shouts. I really wish he would look at his caller ID before he answers the phone, not after. "Unbelievable. I'll tell him . . . And once again, great work."

"I know. The efficient Corporal Nederfield is solving the case while we stand around doing nothing."

"Actually, the efficient Corporal Nederfield has just made solving the case a bit more complicated. She has a make on two of the remaining sets of prints."

"And?"

"Unbelievable."

"Josh, you are repeating yourself. What's unbelievable?" I think he is relishing the fact that he knows something that I don't.

"Let's go back to your trailer," Sheriff McCarthy suggests in a non suggestive tone of voice. I am glad my mobile palace is only a short walk away; otherwise I might have to strangle the Sheriff of Orange County.

CHAPTER ELEVEN

I am tempted to have a beer and call it a day, but it is only 3 o'clock and we aren't any closer to answering the *who* and *why* portions of the equation. I unlock the door to my humble abode on wheels.

"Okay, hot shot, spill the beans. What do you know that I don't and does the information get us closer or further from the end game, which is figuring out who killed young Tyler?" I can't depersonalize him either.

"Here's the latest. Of the three sets of prints, one set belongs to Stephanie Parsons, a real estate broker from Palm Beach. One set remains unidentified and the other set of prints belongs to Monica LeMont, Mildred Letterbaum and Mary Lewiston."

I think my poker face has failed me. "What are you saying?"

"A set of prints belongs to the same person with three different aliases."

Josh is being so matter-of-fact that I want to scream, but instead I say, "At least she has the same initials."

"Corporal Nederfield is trying to get some background on Monica et. al. However, Stephanie Parsons is a bit of a wild card. She is the former wife of one of the partners of the senior Charles Tyler, as well as a big shot in the Palm Beach scene. I definitely need some paper." Our esteemed Sheriff is frothing at the bit-so to speak.

"*What a revoltin' development this is,*" I adroitly add to the conversation. "We now have seven, sets of identified prints, one not yet identified and a bunch of partials. One set is mine and another belongs to Freddy Booker and we have prints from Chip Taylor. So we have five suspects . . . Correct?"

"What if the killer wore latex gloves or some of the partials belong to the killer, but we can't identify them?" The Sheriff is clearly troubled.

"At least we need to try and deal with the four people we know." I don't have a sense of direction.

"Let's get that paper and make a chart connecting everyone together as closely as possible."

I open what passes as my desk drawer, remove a pad of yellow legal paper and hand it the anxiously awaiting Orange County Sheriff.

After about five minutes, Josh produces a chart with five names-the people whose prints we have identified and Chip Taylor and a lot of lines connecting each name.

"Josh, it appears there is a solid line between everyone and young Taylor except Stephanie Parsons; however the old man has a solid line between everyone. Monica is connected only to both Tylers. Bill Clifford is connected to everyone but Monica and Stephanie Powers. Stephanie Powers is connected to everyone but Monica and Clifford. Want my conclusion?"

"Yes please, you deductive reasoning super sleuth," Josh quips.

"I think we need to attach a possible motive to each line. Maybe multiple motives."

"Let's start with Ms. Powers. As far as we know her relationship with Taylor the Elder is financial having to do with her or her former husband's business dealings. Same with Clifford, but a little more solid, since he was the accountant."

"I think being the accountant may have a lot to do with it. If Clifford uncovered really bad business practices, both senior Tyler and possibly Ms. Parsons could be affected," I suggest.

"True, but Clifford wasn't the victim and so if he was blackmailing Tyler, for example, it would be a good motive . . . For his death." Josh is right. I need to concentrate on motive to kill young Tyler.

"Monica would have no motive to kill Chip. He was her meal ticket."

"Well Sherlock, let me suggest that Monica and Mr. Tyler senior seem a bit cozier than one would expect," Sheriff McCarthy postulates.

"I am not following you Josh. If Monica and Chip's father were close, too close, it would be a motive for Chip to kill Monica or his father."

"Unless Monica was trying to break off her relationship with young Tyler in favor of old Tyler and they had a fight." Josh seems to be reaching.

"Thin, but better than nothing. Other than Tyler ruining the race, what motive would Clifford have?" I ask.

"That's where Corporal Nederfield comes in . . . The connection between Clifford and the Tylers on the business side. Same with Ms. Parsons, although that seems a bit more remote unless she had independent business dealings with either Tyler . . . Father or son."

"I think that we also need a little more background on Monica one . . . Two . . . And three."

Sheriff McCarthy already has his cell phone in his hand.

"Corporal, I have a couple of quick areas of inquiry. If you need backup, call Sergeant Mueller. He should be on duty today. Get him into the office. I need his computer skills to run complete background checks on Stephanie Parsons, who seems to be the wild card in this mess. I want everything that might connect her to the decedent or any of the suspects. Something more than her ex-husband and Tyler are or were partners in one or more deals. I want dates, times, places and whether money is a motive. Same with Clifford. There's something going on between these folks. I also want everything thing on Monica or whoever she is. Too many threads, not enough needles. Do you have anything for us? I'm going to speaker."

"Gentlemen, I have the preliminary toxicology report. Tyler had consumed what seems to be about three glasses of wine within about five hours or so of his death. Nothing else. Neither dirty glasses nor a wine bottle was found in the RV. We just got into his phone and are matching both incoming and outgoing calls with names from the phone's own directory and the Ma Bell data base. We may have trouble with some of the cell carriers, but we are working on it. The voice mail will be available for review within a few minutes. I need to get changed to be there at 5, but will have all the call logs by then."

"Olivia," I begin, "we or I should say I am having a hard time coming up with a motive for murder. Usually it is things like blackmail, jealously, hatred or revenge. I just don't see it yet."

"Sometimes it is right in front of your nose, but it takes a while to see it." Corporal Nederfield is talking in rhymes. Or is she?

The Sheriff takes the cell off speaker and says, "Good work, Corporal. Are there any partial prints that don't match the complete prints? I want to reduce the number of suspects, if possible. There are too many already. Thomas will meet you at registration at 5 o'clock. Thanks." Josh returns his phone to his pocket.

CHAPTER TWELVE

"Shit! I forgot to call back Bill Clifford about the call he got from Tyler Senior."

"Thomas, I want to think about how to approach him. Why are his prints in the RV and is there another connection between him and the decedent other than car racing?"

"I guess the esteemed Sheriff of Orange County is allowed to make a good point from time to time."

"It's about time," Josh says a little too quickly. I think is he concerned that there are simply a lot of connecting lines, which means a lot of potentials miscreants.

"It's a beautiful day, let's walk around and get inspired," I suggest. "Maybe even listen to some country and western music."

"We really can't do too much until we know about prints, Miss Monica, phone calls and . . . Now what did I forget? Who killed the kid?"

"You are dripping with sarcasm my old friend," I reply.

"I thought it was good old perspiration. Don't you have AC in your palace?"

"Open the window and let the gentle Florida zephyrs flow through." I can be sarcastic, too.

"Let's check out the scene at the concert, although I can't imagine yet another connection to the decedent."

"Josh, you forgot we still have one set of unidentified finger prints. Maybe someone from the concert crowd. Just as likely as someone from the race crowd."

"Mr. Smarty Pants, you have just added another dimension to this already messed up mess." Sheriff McCarthy opens the trailer door and steps out into the brutal sunlight. "Thomas, I don't like the direction in which this is heading."

"And what direction is that?" I ask

"More factors are coming into play than are being eliminated. I actually don't want to hear from Corporal Nederfield. I am afraid that the call log will be a nightmare."

Within a nano-second, the Sheriff's phone rings. I know he is flummoxed; he even looks at the caller ID.

"We were just talking about you," Josh says. "I am putting you on speaker."

"Hello, Olivia."

"Hello, Thomas. Lots to report."

"It's only been fifteen minutes," Sheriff McCarthy says a little too sharply.

"Sorry Boss, but it's important."

"Sorry Corporal," the Sheriff begins. "I am getting frustrated."

"Thomas, better get him sitting down," she begins. "First, there are over forty sets of clearly identifiable prints, all belonging to the gang of four, except for one set."

"I guess Freddie, Master Tyler and I aren't part of the *gang*."

"Shut up Thomas," Josh shouts. "Go ahead Corporal."

"There are over 200 partials which can be identified as coming from the same sources, including the mystery set. The bad news is that there are three partials which don't come from any of the prints and each of the partials comes from a separate source."

"Correct me if I am wrong, Olivia, but that means the gang of four is now the gang of eight, four of whom we cannot identify . . . Correct?" I hear the Sheriff moaning.

"That's what it means," she answers.

"Is there any good news?" Our not so happy Sheriff asks.

"We got the call logs and for the period of 48 hours before his death, he made or received 22 calls ranging in time from almost an hour to less than thirty seconds. His voice mail had three messages; two from his father saying *call me* and one from his dentist reminding him of an appointment next Tuesday. Some of the calls he made may have gone into the recipient's voice mail. We are working on that. Sheriff McCarthy, I am not sure we need a subpoena for the phone records since I can ID each call in and each call out, except three. Of the known calls, all but two are on the *gang of four* list. No calls from or to Bill Clifford. I am trying to get fingerprints for the two calls and compare them to the partials. I am sure you don't want to add more names to our ever growing suspect pool."

"Are you intentionally keeping us in suspense, Olivia?"

"Do you mean about the ID of the mystery two callers . . . Actually one caller and one callee." The gorgeous Corporal Nederfield is toying with us.

"Olivia, your employer is in a very bad frame of mind and I think it would behoove us all if you simply disclose the two additional suspects," I calmly say.

"Callee #1 is Donald Bradshaw."

"That ambulance chasing, blood sucking lawyer who advertises all over TV?" I think the Sheriff has a strong opinion about the aforementioned ambulance chasing, blood sucking, publicity grabbing, shyster. I guess I do as well.

"Caller #1 is Emily Lange," Corporal Nederfield continues.

"The weather lady from Channel 5?" Our esteemed leader shakes his head in disbelief.

"Yes, Sir."

"Corporal, I know you have got to get down here in . . . A little over an hour, but I want you to try and get prints of those two and compare them to the unknown set and the partials. They probably both have firearms permits so it should be easy. Also, can you make a couple of copies of the call log? Thanks."

"Gotcha. Thomas, see you at five at the track's registration booth. Bye." She hangs up.

"Let's stroll over to the music venue," Josh says.

"Okay," I lamely reply. "Any particular reason?"

"I like county music," the Sheriff of Orange County matter-of-factly says.

CHAPTER THIRTEEN

The promoters of the country and western festival set up the venue in a semi-circle in the track infield with the stage at the open end and with everything else and everybody else filling every remaining square inch. I am not really good at estimating crowds, but there are at least twenty thousand folks watching the concert and another ten thousand watching the races. The crowds often intermingling since a single general admission ticket allows a person open access. Great for fans, lousy for cops trying to solve a murder.

"Ton of people," Josh says. "Bet there is close to twenty thousand."

Not too bad of a guess on my part. Buck Tillotson, who has been around like forever closes his set with his signature song all about beer, babes (his word not mine), broken hearts and blazin' fast cars. Until about five years ago, I was never a country fan. I guess the songs all sounded the same and were depressing. The new country sound is more a fusion of pop, R and B and traditional C and W. I can even understand most of the words and the tunes are very-contemporary.

Our press credentials allow us to freely roam around. Once the stage changeover is completed, the announcer tells us that the next group, the *Golden Doodles*, was just recognized as the top new group by *Country Weekly Magazine*. We have either come a long ways or regressed even more when a group is named after a designer dog, but then again, one of the most popular rap musicians is named *Pit Bull*-so there. I guess I am not surprised that the four band members, two women and two men, are all blonde. They actually are very good.

"Josh, I know you are having the time of your life, but I've got to meet Olivia in a half hour."

"Yup," he grunts in reply.

"Don't you think we have had a long enough recess? Time to get back to class." I am concerned about the lack of progress we are making. Wait a minute! I am only a special deputy first class, or something, and Josh is the actual, in the flesh, Sheriff of Orange County. Why should I be concerned if he's not?

"Thomas, I've been thinking about my chart. I have a bad feeling that the decedent and the original gang of four are each connected to all the others. Some connections we know, others are guesses, but sure as the Lord made little green apples, there is a connection and . . . " The Sheriff is interrupted by his phone ringing. He immediately pushes the speaker function on his cell. "What do you have Corporal?"

"Two quickies, but I think they are important for you two to think about before I get to the track. The previously unidentified set matches the weather reporter, but none matches Attorney Bradshaw. And no luck on the partials. That leaves us with five people whose prints we can identify, all of whom were in the RV and I would say recently because they are fresh, that is they were on top of other prints, long ago smudged. I'm bringing copies of the phone logs. Anything else before I leave?"

"Nope. Nice work." Sheriff McCarthy is not overly loquacious.

"Now what?" I ask.

"If I add Emily Lange to my chart, I have fewer connections, rather than more. I don't think I have enough right now to add the shyster."

"Let's go back to basics. We want to know *who*, but I think that *why* is the linchpin."

"I more or less agree. What's the motive? I think that we should have a chat with Chief Steward Clifford as soon as the last race is over and before the banquet. I need to get a sense whether he is friend or foe." Sheriff McCarthy starts to stroke his chin, again. It's a habit he has had ever since I can remember. It means *stay clear while I do some heavy conjuring*. And I do for about five minutes as we walk back toward the race car side of the facility.

"I am not sure I agree. I can call Bill Clifford. He has been antsy to talk about the calls he has gotten from Tyler the Elder. However, his business connection to old man Tyler, his fingerprints and his obvious *no lost love* of Chip Tyler, still puts him high on the list."

"Yup," our talkative Sheriff replies.

"What are we missing?" I ask no one in particular.

"I'm hung up on the reason someone would kill the kid."

"I have a couple of thoughts. If we apply traditional motivation for murder to your chart, it might strengthen or weaken the likelihood the person stabbed young Tyler."

"There are about ten basic motives for murder. If we eliminate war or terror, so-called mercy killing and reckless and random actions, we are left with anger, including jealously, revenge, humiliation and obsession, money or greed, which might include blackmail, a drug deal, and personal safety. The latter is clearly out; one does not get stabbed in the back or stab someone in the back for personal safety."

"Wait a minute Josh! We have overlooked the obvious . . . *How*. Since he had a knife in his back, we simply assumed he died by being stabbed. However, we haven't asked more about the specifics. Was he stabbed by a right handed person or a person taller than he? Did the nature of the stab wound require great strength?"

Sheriff McCarthy already has his cell phone open. "Have you left yet?"

He pushes the speaker button.

"I'm almost ready to leave . . . Home, not the office. Have you glanced at your watch? It's a quarter to five and I'm twenty minutes away at best," Corporal Nederfield answers.

"Sorry," the Sheriff demurely responds. "Something just came up. Since I am on speaker, I will acknowledge that this is Thomas' brain storm, which I should have thought about. Did anyone analyze the knife wound? Angle of entry?"

"Shit! I was so wrapped up in the fingerprints and phone call stuff that I didn't really read the initial death report. I'll call the M. E.'s office from my car on the way to the track. I'll have the information for you when I get there. How could I have overlooked such an obvious piece of data?"

"Don't get too upset, Olivia," I reply. "Neither the Boss nor his special deputy first class thought of this until about five minutes ago."

"Thanks Thomas. You're a dear."

"You're a dear," Josh silently mimics.

"I'll meet you a little after five," I tell her.

Corporal Nederfield ends the call.

"Not one more word", I say to Sheriff McCarthy holding up my hand like a crossing guard.

"My lips are sealed," he retorts, twisting his fingers on his lips. "Cross my heart." He immediately starts to laugh.

"Stop acting like a ten year old."

"Why?"

"Because."

"Because why?"

"Because I say so."

"You sound like my mother."

"God forbid."

We both are laughing hysterically.

CHAPTER FOURTEEN

"Thomas, I think we should defer any conversation with any suspect until we have the coroner's report," Josh says wiping tears from his eyes.

"Agreed. I better get going. I have to hike up to registration. I'll meet you at the concession stand in about a half hour. Hopefully you will be able to hook up with Freddy."

"I'm going to work on my chart a little bit more, then I'll mosey over. See you in a bit."

"Push the door lock on the castle before you leave."

"Hey, I'm a cop. I know those things."

The day's racing activities are concluding. A lot of cars are already being put away for the evening. Depending where on the net disposable income totem pole you fall, your car is covered with a basic tarp, covered by a fitted car cover, moved under a tent, moved by others under a large tent/awning with other similar cars or moved by others into a huge trailer, undoubtedly air conditioned. The drivers are either sweating profusely or watching their crew sweat profusely. This is Florida, remember?

In so many aspects of the sport, there have been huge changes. Not just with technology, but with attitude. I remember as a boy, when my folks would take me to races, most cars were brought to the track on open trailers-many built in the driver's back yard. I guess that is because we attended mostly "amateur" events. Local people racing their own cars for fun and an occasional trophy or kiss on the cheek from the homecoming queen. It made no difference whether you drove stock cars, modifieds, drag cars or sports cars. It was strictly low budget fun racing. The drivers were often their own mechanics. And everyone was friendly.

There were the professionals who frequented the big name tracks, with sponsorship, tractor trailers with every imaginable piece of equipment and of course-groupies, but for most of us regular people, going to a professional event was simply out of our price range. Anyway, we had a great time doing what we did. Met great people, learned a lot and later on, drank a great deal of beer.

I am not sure when the lines became blurred. It was most obvious in sports car racing, and vintage racing in particular, as "baby boomers" thought that car racing would be a cool hobby. They had money, but few hands on mechanical skills, so lots of small shops specializing in car preparation and track support suddenly appeared. I think this phenomenon was more obvious in the eastern half of the country, since speed shops have always been part of the car crazy California culture. In any event, I saw changes-big changes.

The most obvious of which is that now everyone arrives with their car or cars *snug as a bug in a rug* in large enclosed trailers, with awnings, generators and winches-very often with a professional mechanic.

Car values soared and competition became much more intense as these new-old drivers applied their *do the deal at all cost* mentality to the racing arena. Cars were being pushed beyond the skill level of the drivers and modified way beyond their original configuration. Fortunately, there has been a push back from that attitude-somewhat. The older drivers are getting older and younger participants are being encouraged to compete. Money is still being tossed around like confetti, but the new batch of drivers are racing to relax and trying to distance themselves from the hedge fund mindset. That's why these mixed venues events are becoming more popular and the organizers are actively working to bring family back into the sport. But heck, these are only my thoughts and what else have I got to do while trekking back up to the registration booth. I have been passed by no less than a dozen golf carts, most with an empty seat, but no one has stopped to ask if I wanted a lift. So much for family friendly.

I hope that Freddy doesn't add to our ever increasing suspect pool. Wouldn't it be great if the medical examiner says that a six foot tall, left handed person weighing at least 200 pounds thrust the knife into Chip's back. It eliminates everyone we have on the short list except Bill Clifford, who just doesn't seem the type to murder someone. I wonder if he is even left handed.

I suddenly ask myself, *self, what kind of car does Olivia drive*? Is it a practical, fuel efficient sedan or a practical, but less fuel efficient SUV? I answer my own question as I approach the registration building. Leaning against a classic, bright red, VW convertible beetle is Corporal Nederfield. Very cool with chrome reverse rims, fat tires, stinger exhaust and a red and white tuck and rolled leather interior. I hope my mouth isn't hanging open.

"What did you expect? A little practical sedan or an SUV?" Her smile radiates for miles. I guess my mouth was hanging open.

"Hadn't really given it much thought," I reply unconvincingly.

"I finished restoring this beauty about two years ago and did everything myself except the machine work on the engine and the actual painting," Olivia proudly announces. "My Dad was a mechanic at a Mercedes dealership in Rochester, New York when I was growing up. He came to the U.S. when he was twenty from a small town in southern Denmark and loved working on cars. When I was young, he took me to races: stock cars, sports cars, drag cars-it didn't matter. In the winter we even watched ice racing. He left the dealership about ten years ago, actually retired, but he couldn't stay away from cars, so he opened a small shop. He specialized in all things German. We found this baby in the garage of the sister of a customer who felt that upstate New York weather was not conducive to a convertible. Since I had been accepted at Florida State University, a convertible fit perfectly into my plans. However, it needed a lot of little things to make my Dad agree that it was safe and reliable, so we made it a project we could do together. He found me a practical, fuel efficient sedan to take to school, which I still have. After four years of college, one year of graduate work, one year at the police academy and three years with the AG's office, Dad and I finally finished. I thought this is the perfect venue for Vanessa."

"Vanessa?" I ask.

"That's her name," Olivia answers.

"But of course. How do you do Vanessa? I'm Thomas."

"You're making fun of me."

"Am not."

"Are too."

"Okay . . . I am. Let's get you registered and a parking pass for Vanessa and get back to Sheriff *hot under the collar* McCarthy."

CHAPTER FIFTEEN

I guess I have been around cars way too much since I first noticed the VW and not the drop dead gorgeous Corporal Nederfield, who is wearing an off-white, scoop necked, silk blouse with ¾ length shelves, highlighted by a simple silver chain, blue jeans and a pair of vintage embroidered cowboy boots. Her blond hair is tied with a turquoise and silver clasp. When I said to dress *understated* so that we could blend in, it didn't occur to me that Olivia could never simple blend in even if she had been wearing a gray sweat suit.

"My . . . Don't you look fantastic this evening," I blurted out with about as much finesse as an elephant sipping tea with the Queen.

"Thank you, Thomas." Her smile could melt even the strongest of men, which I am not. "Let's pick up the credentials and get going. I've got a couple of things to show you."

Olivia gets a press pass and a blue wrist band and Vanessa gets a sticker that makes her an official vehicle of the press corps.

"Would you like to drive?" Olivia asks.

"Maybe later. You get behind the wheel and I'll provide directions."

At least, I have retained enough decorum to open the door. Vanessa roars to life with a . . . Roar. There are Porsches racing this weekend that sound tame compared to Vanessa.

"Her 1600 engine is balanced, lightened with high compressions pistons, much modified cams and heads and a pair of dual 40 IDF Weber carbs. She probably has a conservative 130 horsepower." Corporal Nederfield is obviously proud of her car.

"Move over Herbie . . . Here comes Vanessa," I quip.

"Where to?"

"Down the hill."

"Did you walk up here to meet me?"

"The cable car was broken."

For that remark, I get a punch in the arm. I feign excruciating pain. Olivia leans over and gives me a kiss on the cheek.

"All better?"

"Much." I quickly return to the task at hand because Vanessa has covered the ride down the hill in about a minute as juxtaposed to my twenty minute hike up the hill. "Turn left at the gate and show the guard your wrist band."

We both bare our arms to the attendant, who actually pays more attention to Vanessa than to either Olivia or me (no surprise there).

"Now where?"

"To my castle," I respond. Olivia gives me one of those, *what are you talking about?* looks. "I have a classic Airstream in which I reside while on the road. It's about 200 feet on the left just past the cutoff to the infield where the concert is being held."

"Can we go later on?"

"Only if that ogre gives us time off for good behavior."

"He will. His wife, Cheryl called the office and told me to get him home before 9 o'clock. No excuses. She said he needs to *sleep on it*."

We pull alongside the Airstream. "Welcome to Maison Ballard, mademoiselle".

"Merci." Olivia reaches over the seat and retrieves two shopping bags. "One for me and one for you and Sheriff McCarthy."

"Pardon?"

"You don't think I am going to sit down with you two unless you take a shower and change into, at the very least, a clean shirt, do you?"

"No, ma'am", I sheepishly answer knowing full well that neither Josh nor I has given a shower and a clean shirt a moment's thought.

"I didn't think so. I stopped by the outlet store and bought you each a nice cotton, collared shirt and a bath towel."

I start to sputter something inane, when Josh opens the trailer door. "There you are. You need to get over to the concession stand and meet Freddy."

"Since we're going to dine directly after meeting with Freddie, I think we should take a quick shower and change shirts." I try to make this sound like my idea.

"Huh?"

"Yup."

Olivia opens her bag and hands the Sheriff a mauve polo shirt and a towel and hands me a turquoise shirt and towel. It kind of matches her hair clasp. Do you think she was thinking about that when she bought the shirt?

"And here is a bar of lavender smelling soap. Now march . . . Gentlemen."

Josh stares at me and grunts.

"Oh, Sheriff, your wife said you have to be home at 9 o'clock. She said *no excuses and nothing is going to happen that can't wait until morning.* Chop . . . Chop, we don't want to keep Freddy waiting."

The expression *being sent to the showers* takes on a whole different meaning.

CHAPTER SIXTEEN

I have to admit, the shower feels really great. We even have hot water, which at a race track is an iffy thing. The shirt fits perfectly. How did she know?

"Nice shirt," Josh says running his hands through his rather skimpy head of hair. "Color looks good on you."

"Hey, you look pretty spiffy yourself."

"You can run, but you can't hide. This should also be a lesson to our perp . . . Whoever he is."

"Or she is," I add.

"Yup."

"I think we should talk with Freddy and see how his afternoon has gone and then review what Olivia has brought."

We briskly walk back to the trailer and knock politely.

"Coming," Corporal Nederfield answers. She opens the door and we both audibly gasp. She has run a comb or brush through her hair, touched up a bit of makeup and the result is beyond spectacular. We throw the plastic bag with the towels and dirty shirts into the trailer.

"Whoa, amigos. Towels hung up in the bathroom and dirty shirts can stay in the bag provided it is tightly fastened. Soap?"

"It smelled so good, we left it in the showers for some other stinky guy to use," I answer.

"Very thoughtful. Let's go." She offers us each an arm and like Dorothy, the Scarecrow and the Tin Man, we start down the yellow brick road, although it appears like asphalt to me. Thank goodness, no one starts to sing.

Freddy approaches us in a dead run, pardon the expression.

"You won't believe who I just saw?"

We gaze at each other, mentally assembling a list.

"Emily Lange, the weather lady."

My first thought is *so what?* My second thought is *suspect?* My third thought is *how did Freddy know?*

"Freddy, take a deep breath. I would like to introduce a member of my department, Corporal Olivia Nederfield, who has been doing a lot of behind the scenes work. All the forensic examination has been done under her supervision and we have made a lot of progress, but not enough."

"What is so important about Emily Lange?" I ask.

"When I was doing my inquiry, several people told me they saw her on Friday night here at the track. The blokes recognized her from TV, so it seems to be a solid ID." Before any of us could say anything, Freddy continued, "I once knew a Carl Nederfield. Wonderful chap. Danish. Best damn mechanic on German cars I ever met. Lived somewhere in New York. You know him?" His comments were obviously directed at Olivia.

"He's my father," she proudly answers.

"Is he well?" Freddy asks.

"Very well and it's very kind of you to ask."

"When I first came to the states, I got a job crewing at Watkins Glen for this fellow who had a fast, but very temperamental Porsche. Couldn't get the bloody car to run right. Your Dad was just walking around the paddock. He obviously knew a lot of people. Well, he saw that I was having a rough time of it and ask if he could help. I was grateful. In less time than it's taking to tell the story, he made a couple of adjustments to the carbs, tweaked the timing and viola, perfecto. The owner was ecstatic. He told me that the measure of a good mechanic is to ask for help if it's needed. I never told him I didn't ask for help, but that your Dad offered. In any event, I was employed by that gent for three years before I went out on my own."

During the entire story, Olivia was gently steering Freddy to a picnic table under the concession tent. Very smoothly done.

"Did any of your contacts say exactly when they saw Ms. Lange? Or where they saw her? And whether she was alone or with friends?" The Orange County Sheriff is trying to bring Mr. Hooker back into the investigation.

"Righto. There were several sightings on Friday. One around 2 p.m. and that was corroborated by two different chaps on two different crews."

"Where was Ms. Lange?" I blurt.

"Oh, she was entering the music venue at the entrance quite near Charles' RV."

"Alone?" Sheriff McCarthy asks.

"Each time she was seen, she was alone," Freddy replied. "The next time anyone saw her was about 11 p.m. This time she was outside the concert area, close to some of the larger car transports, just standing there, apparently waiting for someone. Again, she was seen by several people who all agreed on the time and location."

"Well done," Josh says. "Did anyone comment on what she was wearing or whether she seemed disheveled?"

Master mechanic Hooker removes a small notebook from his shirt pocket which he opens. "Out of the five who saw Miss Lange . . . Ms. Lange, only one commented upon her appearance. She was dressed like the average concert-goer. She was wearing a short sleeve blue denim dress. It was very short according to my source, which is probably why he noticed her in the first place. At first, he didn't connect her to the otherwise demur weather reporter. When I just saw her, she had on a flowery sun dress which fell well below the knee. Her hair was tied back, but not severe. I recognized her immediately, but as you know Sheriff McCarthy, I'm good at faces."

"Please explain?" Olivia interjects.

"Our cover was blown immediately after meeting Mr. Hooker because he had seen my mug on TV."

"Good thing, because his investigative skills are quite well honed," Corporal Nederfield responds.

"Does that include observing you and Mr. Ballard in that beautifully restored VW? Bet your Dad had a hand in it."

"His hand guided mine, but he let me skin my knuckles many times."

"Freddy, since we only have about ten more minutes until they raise the cocktail burgee, did you find any murder suspects?" I thought the best way to get a straight answer is to ask a straight question.

"I spoke with probably forty people who knew Master Tyler. They were all candid and forthcoming about their opinions of him. Not high is an understatement. In addition to several profanities, the words, *arrogant*, *disrespectful*, *jerk* and *way over his head* were most often used in description of him. Having said that, no one had a level of animus rising to murder. Perhaps some words or even a shove, but murder . . . Out of the question. I say this because murder requires a motive and no one seemed to really care enough about young Tyler to give him much thought. It seems rather heartless to say, but it seems he wasn't worth talking to, let alone killing."

"Do you have a sense that this attitude was held by most of the members of the racing community?" I know it is asking Freddy to make a broad assumption from a small sampling, but he is in the best position to help us eliminate a whole lot of potential suspects.

"I have been pondering just that, Thomas. One cannot exponentially expand one's findings, but I have been around these folks for decades and find them pretty much as they present themselves. Basically, no bull shit. Pardon me Miss Nederfield."

"Olivia . . . Mr. Hooker."

"Sheriff, I don't think anyone gave a tinker's dam about Charles Tyler, unless, of course, he caused an accident. I guess we are fortunate that his mishaps on the track only did damage to his ego or his own cars."

"Freddy, you have saved us literally weeks of work and hope you will join us for a bite to eat tonight," Sheriff McCarthy says.

"Thank you for the kind invitation. Maybe we'll share a pint after the case is over. Wouldn't be good for my image to be seen with a copper," Freddy Hooker says with a wink. "Cheers!"

He rises and briskly walks away.

CHAPTER SEVENTEEN

"Well, Freddy sure cut to the chase, figuratively speaking," I say staring at the quickly moving backside of the former mechanic of Charles William Tyler III.

"His information was invaluable," Sheriff McCarthy snorts.

"Presuming that one in our existing pool of suspects is the murderer," I retort.

"Gentlemen, I think we should put our efforts into those suspects we can identify rather than looking for a needle in a haystack. Plenty of time for that if we can't close this one out . . . Shortly."

"Does that mean we can have a beer with our food?" I think my question is appropriate.

"We have every reason to believe Bill Clifford will attend and every reason to believe neither Monica nor Tyler the Elder will attend since they are not on the guest list. I never thought of searching for either Stephanie Parsons' name or Emily Lange's name. Corporal Nederfield, do you have photographs of the two?"

"But, of course." Olivia opens her enormous handbag and produces two files. "I made ten copies of each of the photos from their drivers' licenses. Came out quite well."

"What other goodies do you have in that bag?"

"For me to know and you to find out," she quips

"Alright you two, stop the chit chat." The Sheriff can be such a fuddy duddy sometimes. "Do you have the phone records and coroner's report?"

"Yes to the first and not yet to the second."

Josh raises one eyebrow. "Explain . . . Please."

"I called the medical examiner's office as soon as we hung up, but he had just left . . . For a round of golf. His assistant was really upset. She kept on saying *that Saturday is usually his day off, but he came in special for this.* After I calmed her down, she said that he had dictated his findings onto his computer and that Alex, whoever he is, will be recreating the murder scene with animation. It should be ready for review later tonight. The M.E. is apparently going back to the office to review it and make any changes which might be required and e send it to both the Sheriff and to me. Apparently the animation will be a graphic representation of the actual crime based on the forensic evidence. Pretty cool stuff." Olivia peers up at me and continues, "Which brings us back to Thomas' question."

"Which one?" The Sheriff of Orange County has a very short attention span.

"The one about beer," Olivia and I reply in unison.

"We still need to still deal with Clifford, Ms. Lange and possibly Ms. Parsons," Our esteemed Sheriff reminds us.

"Why don't we mingle, with a beer, so we won't be too conspicuous? Let's see what we can see. I am sure that Bill Clifford will track us down and ask us about his calls from Tyler the Elder. Emily Lange . . . I'm not sure. And Stephanie Parsons is a long shot. Freddy virtually eliminated the hordes." I am not getting a reaction from Josh. He starts his chin stroking.

"Corporal Nederfield, what do you think?"

"For one, if we are truly trying to pass ourselves off as press corps, no offense Thomas, you have got to call me Olivia and I can call you ... Just about anything but Sheriff McCarthy. Secondly, I would like to mingle. I am curious about Emily Lange's presence at the track. She doesn't seem like the car type. Also, I think seeking out Ms. Parsons would behoove us. Toward Clifford, we should be non-committal until we review the medical findings. Last, but not least, the phone logs need to be reviewed in meticulous detail so we can narrow the time window. I am somewhat doubtful that the recordings of the voice messages left by Tyler will be available any time soon. However, based on the length of time of each call he made, I think he actually talked with the intended person. Bottom line, there's not a lot we can do tonight, except get some cold beer and warm food."

"Josh ... Call me Josh."

"Since that crisis is now averted, I suggest we search for both Ms. Parsons and Ms. Lange ... And let's get that cold beer," I propose.

"Corporal . . . Olivia . . . May I have a copy of the Stephanie Parsons' picture. Do you have her vitals?"

"She's 45 years old, divorced with one grown daughter who lives in Arizona. Five foot six inches tall and her weight is listed at 130 pounds. Based on her picture, that may be fairly accurate."

"Are we being catty?" I quip.

"Just giving the facts and only the facts," Olivia retorts.

"Would you two cut that out?" Ooops. Not good to get the Big Guy angry.

"Eyes blue and hair black. Her address is Palm Beach. Nice section. All condos. Has a real estate broker's license. Her ex was a partner of the elder Tyler. He wasn't a major player, but was always in for a piece of the action. Kenneth

Parsons is still listed as a limited partner on most of Tyler's deals. I would say he is very comfortable, but not in the same league as Tyler," Olivia continues.

"So one could assume that Ms. Parsons is also comfy, correct?" I am not sure where I am going with this, but something doesn't fit with my journalistic order of things. An attractive, based on the photo, not quite cougar, well off woman in the RV of handsome, early 30's son of her former husband's business partner? Something is rotten in the state of Denmark. Shit! That could have been a like major faux pas if I had said that out loud. Glad I talk to myself . . . A lot.

"Are you alright, Thomas? You just had a weird expression on your face," Olivia asks.

"Get used to it. He always has weird expressions on his face."

"Thanks Josh. Let's get going. We can cut through the paddock to get to the hospitality tent."

Once again, the three of us start down the yellow brick road, arm in arm.

CHAPTER EIGHTEEN

The line to get into the food tent, wherein an ice cold beer lurks in waiting, is moving quickly. I am clutching our guest passes to present to whoever is checking for gate crashers. Probably not a good choice of words for race car drivers. Approaching the check in table I hear,

"Thomas, I have been trying to get a hold of you all day."

"Bill, it's been crazy. We'll touch bases as soon as we check in and get settled. Watch for us." I wave somewhat lacklusterly.

"Your names?" A voice from the check-in table asks.

"McCarthy, Ballard and Nederfield," I respond without thinking.

"Are you with a car?"

"No, we are with the press." I answer. Then it occurs to me.

"Gotcha. Go right in." The check-in lady smiles.

"Do you have the names of all the people who are coming to tonight's event?" I try to sound professionally journalistic. "Obviously we are doing a story on the race and the attendees at tonight's wonderful event would be a great addition to our story."

"Gee, I'd like to help, but I can't give you our list. I need to check in everyone."

"Yes, I understand, but could I look at it?"

"I would have to ask my superiors," the check-in lady replies.

"Can you do so . . . Now?" I am trying to be polite, without appearing too anxious.

"Gee, there are a lot of people in line."

I am almost out of *niceties* when our beloved Sheriff, who is getting somewhat hot under the collar, says "in the interest in getting everyone checked in as quickly as possible, I need to see your list . . . Now."

"I don't like your attitude," the check-in lady says. "I am going to have to call security."

Josh and Olivia pull their badges from their back pockets, show them to the check-in lady and say together, "We are security!"

I do not like to show my special deputy badge for fear that people will start laughing. However, our check-in lady seems more like she is going to have a heart attack.

I say in as calm a voice as I can, "Please, this will only take a second. We know what we are looking for."

Suddenly from behind me, a voice shouts, "Is there a problem here?"

Josh, Olivia and I all swivel to the left to see the source of the imperiousness question. Holy smokes . . . Guess who? Charles William Tyler, Jr. in the flesh with a way too young lady next to him. Monica?

"No problem sir," Sheriff McCarthy draws himself up to the top of his 6'3" frame. "I am the Sheriff of Orange County and I would like to take a quick glance at the guest list for this event."

"Sheriff McCarthy, I am Charles Tyler and I own this property and without a search warrant, I think you are out of bounds."

"Corporal Nederfield, how long will it take to get a search warrant?" Josh is really getting worked up.

Tyler the Elder backs down a bit and says, "We are always willing to assist the members of the law enforcement community. May I ask what this is about?"

Since I never know what our esteemed Sheriff might say, I interject, "Mr. Tyler, we want to make sure that the venue is safe."

"And who are you?" He retorts.

I can see why Josh wants to strangle this guy, he's an arrogant jackass. I remove my badge from my jeans and put it so close to Tyler's face that he can't read the *special* part. I immediately return it to my pocket.

"Sorry . . . Sir. Feel free to examine the list."

"Can you make us a copy?" Olivia is glaring at Tyler the Elder. "So we can examine it more closely . . . Later?"

"Of course! I'll have it printed right now."

I have always been a kind soul, but if Tyler were lying in the gutter I would . . .

Sheriff Josh spins the check-in list toward him and he and Olivia start going through the names. There's not enough room for the three of us to go over the list, so I direct my comment to Mr. Tyler's companion. "Hi, my name is Thomas Ballard. Sorry for any inconvenience."

She answers, "Hi. My name is Monica LeMont. Charles can get upset real quick. He's got a temper, you know."

"This is just routine. We don't want to have someone who shouldn't be here." I am beginning to talk like her.

"Thank you Mr. Tyler. We have been on high alert at major venues and we err toward caution." Josh McCarthy just delivered the biggest lie, but I think that Tyler bought it. He has moved up a couple of notches on the suspect ladder.

And Monica? Where do I begin? She gives me goose bumps the way she purrs instead of speaks.

"Glad to see vigilance, even though it can seem invasive," Mr. Tyler responds. He is scanning the huge tent while talking to us. "Do either of you know my son, Chip? I can't seem to find him although he's supposed to be here. His rig was driven away earlier today. Maybe he had mechanical problems that couldn't be fixed at the track."

Tyler the Senior is asking and answering his own questions. I can't tell if there is concern in his voice or annoyance that the heir apparent isn't around. And then again, there's Monica. I need a beer more than ever.

Josh is handed a large white envelope by one on the guest-list checkers. "It's the names of everyone attending this evening's event," she breathlessly says. Obviously when Mr. Tyler wants something, everyone jumps.

"Thank you," he curtly, but graciously answers. He turns-we follow. We move from the ante-tent to a tent that would make P. T. Barnum smile. The cacophony of sounds is almost as loud as the big block boys at full throttle. The place is jammed with car folks. We will be lucky to find each other let alone our cast of suspects. We shoulder our way towards one of many beer stands.

"Olivia, what would you like to drink?" I politely shout above the din.

She gives a quick look at Josh, who nods and in a most authoritative gesture, holds up three fingers. It takes a wiggle and a hip check or two to actually reach the bar, but three cold beers await. I push a couple of dollars into the tip jar, hand Olivia a beer, hand Josh a beer and grab the remaining cup and start to back out of the throng that has formed behind us. I don't want to spill a drop since it may be a while before I'll be able to return.

CHAPTER NINETEEN

After bobbing and weaving through the crowd, we finally find a space where we can talk-and drink.

"Very interesting," I begin. "But definitely strange."

"You mean strange that the decedent's father is with Monica . . . Whoever? Or strange because their names are not on the guest list? Or strange that in addition to Clifford's name appearing on the guest list, the names of Ms. Lange and Ms. Parsons appear? Or strange that the name of . . . Attorney Donald Bradshaw is on the guest list?" Orange County Sheriff McCarthy certainly has my attention.

"All of the above," I sputter. I wish I had been able to see over their shoulders when they were examining the list. I'm glad we got a copy. I wonder if there are any other surprises.

"Gentlemen, we need a game plan," Olivia suggests and then takes a long sip of beer. "I suggest that we separate, circulate and meet back here in a half hour. I sense that we should stake out a table as well. Thomas, do you have any business cards?"

"Sure. Why?"

"I want to put three cards at a table to reserve our seats, preferably one with a view of the whole tent. Using our cards would be a bad idea. The press gets to eat . . . And observe. We only get to serve . . . And protect."

Josh nods. "You guys find a table. I'll start to circulate. Thirty minutes . . . Right here."

I wonder if the police academy teaches you to use as few words as possible to convey a thought. Sheriff McCarthy has mastered the skill.

At first I try to walk next to Olivia in our efforts to get to the ideal table which I see across the tent-far corner-close to food and beverage-close to an exit-and empty. The tent is even more crowded than a few minutes before. Race car people love free food. I finally give up, grab Olivia's hand and start to wedge an opening. Some success, but not a lot.

"Let me try," the lovely Corporal Nederfield whispers in my ear. I shrug. Whatever I am attempting isn't working. "Excuse me . . . Excuse me", Olivia says in a voice somewhat between Marilyn Monroe and Clint Eastwood. The crowd moves aside like Moses parting the Red Sea.

"I'm impressed," I tell her as we reach our table.

"Lots of experience," she replies.

I am not sure how to take that comment, but it works.

Olivia places my three cards in front of three chairs and moves the chairs so that they are leaning against the table. She opens her rather large hand bag, which probably has a gun, taser and handcuffs inside. She removes a lipstick case and writes "*PRESS*" on the paper tablecloth. "That should do it. Let's mingle."

This lady is amazing, resourceful and very pretty. Great combination. And she likes cars. The only drawbacks are that she is a cop and I don't know if there is a *somebody* in her life. *Carpe diem*. We start our search for-whatever. Finding Ms. Parsons and Ms. Lange should be easier than finding Bradshaw, since the ratio of men to women is about 6 to 1.

Actually the ratio of men to women under the age of 50 is about 25 to 1. As luck may have it, we spot the ambulance chaser almost immediately. Not only is his face plastered over the highways and byways of Central Florida, it is almost impossible to watch TV without seeing him tell you how *each client is his most important client.* Also pink pants and a pale blue shirt at a banquet for a vintage car race kind of jumps right out at you. Lilli Pulitzer would shutter in her grave at the sight. Bradshaw is *holding court*, waving his hands around the air as he speaks. I have often wondered what a killer might look like. Pink and blue-no. However, since we have not made a lot of progress on motive-maybe. Because he is so obnoxious and for no other reason-definite maybe.

"Thomas, please restrain me." I give Olivia a look. "I have an urge to rush us to Attorney Bradshaw and tell him that he is irresistible in pink and I want him . . . As my lawyer."

Heads turn toward us as I begin to laugh uncontrollably. Suddenly, I feel a powerful hand on my shoulder. "You are not being respectful. He's absolutely perfect in pink." It's Sheriff McCarthy's turn to laugh.

Fortunately the crowd closes it ranks again before anyone recognizes us-well Josh. "One suspect ID'd," I say.

"Actually three. I saw Clifford. He was talking to some other car guys dressed in white and Emily Lange is doing something with a TV camera over near the stage."

"Actually five," Olivia says. "Don't forget, we saw the senior Tyler and the girl friend. Exactly whose girl friend is still up in the air?"

"That leaves us but one . . . Stephanie Parsons," I note. Whereupon, I feel a tap upon my shoulder, this time with substantially less force.

"Did you mention my name?" a rather attractive, but very drunk woman announces.

"Why yes . . . I did. I was commenting upon the resurrection of the Lilly Pulitzer look in Palm Beach," snidely referring to the *shyster*. "And my friend here, Mr. McCarthy, has been talking about possibly buying something in Palm Beach . . . Second home. I recalled hearing your name from a fellow who does some development in South Florida and . . . Like magic you're here." That was probably the biggest line of BS that I have told in years, but I told it eloquently and more importantly, believably, especially to an inebriated listener. I don't feel a bit ashamed. There is still a killer on the loose and drunk or sober, Ms. Parsons is on the short list.

Josh quickly picks up his end and offers her his hand. "Hi, I'm Josh McCarthy. Nice to meet you."

"I'm so rude. My name is Thomas Ballard and this is my dear friend, Olivia."

"Are you a car guy? Like don't you write about cars?" Ms. Parsons asks.

"Why yes, I am." I give her my most charming smile. Well, maybe my second most charming smile. I am saving the best for *my dear friend* . . . Later.

"Have you seen him?" Ms. Parson is about six inches from me. She doesn't smell of booze, so I suspect that vodka is the culprit.

"To whom do you refer?" Why am I trying to sound grammatically correct to someone who is six sheets to the wind?

"Why Charlie Tyler, that's whom," she replies, slightly slurring her words.

"We saw him at the registration table a little while ago," I respond.

"No, not him! His son, the race car driver."

Three mouths suddenly opened, but not a sound uttered forth.

Since I have been the blabber mouth, I decide to push for some more information. Shock is often the best tool. "I saw him leave in his RV towing the car trailer earlier this morning." Absolute truth.

"No, that's not possible! He said he'd be here!" Stephanie Parsons is starting to panic.

"When did you last speak to him?" Olivia asks in a voice far more soothing that mine.

"I saw him last night. He'd had a bad day with the car. He was very angry. But he can be such a child at times." I am not sure what I am hearing. A suspect admitting she was at the scene of the crime at about the time the crime was committed. However, we have been a bit deceitful about who we are and she is definitely impaired. Wouldn't hold up in court.

"Maybe young Tyler has returned," Sheriff McCarthy says. He is going somewhere, but I am not sure where. "Would you like me to walk around the tent with you and see if we can find him?" Slick, old buddy, very slick. If they run into Tyler the Senior and Monica, I think their collective reactions might be interesting, especially if you're thinking what I am thinking.

CHAPTER TWENTY

I feel the ebb and flow of the now assembled mass of attendees at this evening's feast. For safety reasons, but of course, I grab Olivia's hand as we mingle. "Where are we going?" I ask.

"I'm not sure. I thought you had a plan," She replies.

"Who should we be looking for?" Yet another question.

"All of the suspects are accounted for. I think we should get some hors d'oeuvres and go back to the table. There's too much noise for us to talk."

"Follow me, oh beautiful princess." I make a slashing gesture and start to move toward one of the food stations set up throughout the tent, Olivia in tow. For me, nobody moves. I slip and slide amongst the crowd and try not to spill any beer, especially on my new shirt. "Hark, my fair maiden . . . Sustenance awaits at yonder table."

"Thomas, promise me one thing," Olivia says.

"For you . . . Anything."

"Don't give up your day job and become an actor." The lovely Corporal is radiating mirth.

"I get it. Sure pop my dream bubble of the footlights on Broadway," I answer.

Since Olivia and I are almost the same height, she simply leans over and gives me a cheek kiss. "I'm hungry," she says.

We find ourselves in a quickly moving line of others with the same idea-food. The presentation is actually quite nice. Although there is an element of self service, the several large roasts of beef and turkey are tended by a server who slices each of us a heaping portion-with a very large knife-much like the one I saw protruding from Chip Tyler's back. I gaze over at Olivia who appears to be thinking the same thing.

Rather than challenge the crowd with both a plate and a beer in hand, we elect to go outside the tent a circle the perimeter until we get to our table.

"Thomas!" Olivia nudges me with her shoulder. "It's Emily Lange."

The local weather person is interviewing two men-wearing matching linen blazers, beige pants and bright solid-colored shirts. They have that GQ image. Drivers? Owners? Both? Even the ear studs in their ears match. Last night at Volusia Speedway all the men wore matching attire as well; greasy blue jeans, tee-shirts and ratty sneakers. It's the racing, not the clothes that *makes the man* or woman.

"She appears to be working." Olivia awakens me from yet another aside. "I think we should keep an eye on her and have a chat . . . Later."

"Good idea. Let's find our table. I am starving."

"And the poor boy must keep up his strength, mustn't he?" Why does this beautiful cop keep picking on me? Well, teasing me. Because I am a sensitive kind of guy and an easy target-and hungry.

Our table or what I had called our table is filled with folks-talking, eating and drinking. Fortunately, the group, identified by their matching shirts, respected our space, although it appears that they moved a few chairs from an adjoining table.

"May we join you?" I ask

"If you are Thomas Ballard you may, but your companion may join us even if you are not Thomas Ballard," one of the group answers.

"Lucky me, and I am Thomas Ballard and this is Olivia Nederfield. We hope to be joined by a third member of our team, who was last seen with an attractive, but very drunk lady clinging to him."

"We are all from the team managing those rather elegant Bentleys that are being displayed at the head of the main straightaway," another group member says. His accent is strange. Clipped, but not British. "I am Hans Leiter and we are planning on driving the three beasts in the pre-war race tomorrow. I will introduce you to our assemblage: Pierre, Franco, Stanford, Frederick, Charles and moi." Each man waves or bows his head as his name is called. "And our team chaperone, Margarite, who is also my wife."

"Bon jour," she says demurely. "You are a writer . . . No?"

"I try."

"And succeed, I might add," Hans interjects. "I have followed your by-line in many magazines and on-line. You are quite good and have a real feel for the sport."

"Thank you. It is my goal to bring the people and the cars alive to those who are not in attendance-where ever the race."

"And you mademoiselle? Are you a writer as well?" Margarite Leiter asks. All sixteen eyes stare at Olivia.

"My role is purely a fact finder. I provide background so that Thomas and Josh, whom I hope returns soon, are able to reach informed conclusions."

"I find that hard to believe," Stanford says, in a heavy Welsh accent. "I saw you this afternoon arrive in a classic beetle. Fact finders are supposed to be inconspicuous."

"It depends on what kind of facts I am searching for. *Skal.*" Olivia lifts the cup of beer to her lips.

"*Cheers, cin cin, santé, prost, bottom's up,*" our mini United Nations of Bentley drivers responds.

"Please eat before it gets too cold," Margarite insists. I can see why Hans referred to her as the *chaperone*. She lifts a wine glass, not the plastic kind, "Peace and happiness."

Olivia and I smile at one another and click plastic cups. "Here's looking at you, kid." Maybe Bogie said it better, but never with more feeling.

CHAPTER TWENTY-ONE

"Dear Lord, I need a drink after that," Josh announces as he returns to the table. "Excuse me," he says to our new friends.

"I understand you have been escorting a rather inebriated woman around the tent. I hope she is presently able to walk alone," Stanford quips. "Leaving her in such a condition is most unchivalrous."

The Sheriff of Orange County blushes-a bit.

"Josh, I want you to meet our table-mates. Olivia had to defend the only remaining chair at the table and we needed to explain your absence." I repeat the names of team Bentley.

"Ms. Parsons is sleeping it off in the track manager's office. I put her there myself." Sheriff McCarthy has been married over thirty years to a wonderful woman and their relationship is rock solid. I think it's funny. He is clearly uncomfortable.

"Mon dieu!" Pierre shouts. "A beautiful lady in the manager's office? What a waste."

"Pierre! Stop that." Margarite slaps him on the shoulder-hard.

"My brother, he is typical Frenchman, which is sometimes not a good thing."

Pierre rises out of his chair and says, "Vive a difference!" He leans over and gives his sister a kiss on each cheek. She slaps him again, but with far less force.

Josh reaches over, grabs my cup of beer and drains it. "All better." Everyone at the table laughs.

"Now I suppose I will have to get myself another beer and probably you want one, too."

"Allow me," Stanford offers. "Need one myself and I'll get one of those wonderful little cardboard cup holders and bring back several. Cheerio." He rises and deftly slides out around the table.

"We need to talk," Josh whispers.

"Later, there are still a few things I want to do here . . . In addition to eating. You've got a little over an hour," I reply.

"What?"

Olivia leans over and points at Sheriff McCarthy's watch. "Home by 9."

Thinking I had better make a show of being a journalist, I ask, to no one in particular, "What do you think of the facilities at Citrus Grove?"

"For vintage racing, I think it is splendid," Hans answers. "The course might have a hard time accommodating super fast cars for long races. Several of the turns are quite tight which necessitates hard braking. An endurance race of twelve or even six hours would take its toll. However, for the senior cars, it is perfect. The straightaway is just long enough and there are numerous spots where passing is possible and safe. At my age, I am most thankful for the non track facilities-like hot showers to which Margarite sent us all before coming here."

Suddenly, I feel a sharp pain caused by being kicked in the ankle by Olivia. I also think she just stuck out her tongue at me. Humph.

Trying to recover my composure I continue, "Do you think sharing the venue with a music festival is distracting or diminishes the experience?"

"That is an interesting question, monsieur," the table's designated chaperone begins. "We have been to many, many race tracks and as a companion and not a driver or a real car aficionado; I think that the addition of music is a wonderful idea. I confess I do not understand your country and western music, but it is a pleasant change from the constant sounds of the race cars. I have twice been over to the stage. I especially like watching the people. They are so much different than the racing menagerie. I am looking forward to listening to music after this event. Right, garcons?" Each of the men at the table nod deferentially. The table becomes very quiet.

"Did I miss something?" Stanford says returning with two not one cardboard trays each holding six beers. A truly death defying act in this crowd. He places the cups in the middle of the table. Removes one each for Josh and me, removes a third and offers it to Olivia, who quickly accepts, takes one for himself and pushes the tray to his remaining teammates."

"Would you like some more wine, Cheri?" Hans asks his wife.

"Oui . . . Merci," She replies.

Hans reaches under the table and places a weather-beaten leather case on the table which he carefully opens. Two bottles of wine are nestled in velvet-one unopened-the other with a small silver stopper. The box also houses a second glass, probably crystal, like the one from which Margarite has been drinking. Very classy and clearly not brought for show, but for function. Hans pours a small amount into the glass, re-corks the bottle, returns it to its nest and hands the glass to his wife. She gives him an adoring smile.

"We were talking about your evening activities before you returned," I pipe in. "A Country and Western concert, I understand."

"My dear Margarite . . . " Stanford begins. "That sounds splendid."

I roll my eyes, but recover enough to say, "May Olivia and I join you? Josh has been summonsed by his wife to return by nine."

"That would be wonderful. Mademoiselle Olivia . . . It's Okay?"

"Madam Leiter, I had already asked Thomas if he would take me to the concert."

"Tres   bon."
"There are a few things I need to do before I can be free. Let's meet at 9:15 at the entrance gate near Paddock A," I propose. I know Josh has something he wants to tell us and I want to chat with or at least observe Emily Lange. And what about Ms. Parsons? I examine my plate, which is empty. The measure of true hunger is eating and not even knowing you have consumed a slap of beef, tucked into a roll with horseradish sauce. Maybe I should get another to make sure I enjoyed it. "Until later." We three rise. I lift my beer and say, "To new friends."

CHAPTER TWENTY-TWO

"Are you going to keep us in suspense all night?" I give the Sheriff a gentle push. Over the years I have learned not to give him a hard push unless you want a hard push back-from a 6'3"-260 pound-grizzly bear.

"She's a wacko."

"Is that an opinion or a medical term?"

"Both. Ms. Stephanie Parsons reminds me of the character from *Play Misty for Me* . . .

"Evelyn," Olivia and I say together.

"Yeh. She is creepy-scary. She is so obsessed with Charles William Tyler III that if she can't have him . . . Nobody can."

"And she doesn't have him?" Olivia adds.

"This is where it gets crazy."

I have never heard Sheriff McCarthy use so many unprofessional words before. He continues, "I sense that they had a brief relationship about a year or so ago. You know, before Monica. It didn't end badly; the decedent simply had his attention diverted."

"The age difference is what . . . Ten years?" This seems to bother Olivia.

"Actually . . . Thirteen, although Ms. Parsons appears very good for her age." I don't think that sounds too chauvinistic.

Olivia gives me one of those looks.

"According to what I could gather from her garbled speech, she always believed that young Tyler would come to his senses and see that she had so much more to offer him than . . . Monica, whom she referred to rather profanely."

"Okay Boss," I begin, "She may have a motive and it sounds like she had the opportunity since she's been at the track and even admitted that she saw Chip the night of his murder."

"Do you think we should go back to the manager's office and try to get her to talk coherently to us?" Corporal Nederfield is focused on Ms. Parsons.

"Yes and no," the Sheriff answers. "Do we have to give her a Miranda warning before we talk to her? Shouldn't we have done so already? Is anything she says admissible? She was drunk as a skunk."

"What if I talk to her . . . Unofficially? The case against her is very circumstantial without her statements. I am aware of the fruit of the poison tree doctrine, so that anything we get based on what she has already said is also tainted. Maybe she can shine a light in a corner we haven't examined." I am grasping for straws.

"What if she is putting on an act? Pretending she's drunk so that everything she says can't be used against her?" While Olivia sounds cynical, what she is saying is possible.

"It wasn't an act," Sheriff McCarthy responds. "I know a real drunk when I see one."

"She could have gotten drunk intentionally," I suggest.

"Makes no difference. Thomas, you check on her, we'll mix. I want to check out the remaining suspects. It may be the last time they are together in one place and except for the killer; no one seems to know if young Tyler is dead or alive."

At least Josh didn't say decedent again. I probably would have screamed.

"When shall we three meet again? In thunder, lightning or in rain?" I hope Shakespeare isn't angered by my rather loose use of the witches of Macbeth.

"Too much knowledge is not a good thing. Right here in one half hour." The Sheriff can say the meanest things.

"Sir, I think I should go with Thomas while you tour the tent. I don't want Ms. Parsons to cause a scene and accuse Thomas of being other than a gentleman. And besides, since he is a special deputy . . . "

"First class," I interrupt.

"First class," Olivia repeats with deference, "He is actually representing your office."

"Good point. One half hour . . . Here." The Orange County Sheriff has officially ended this conversation. He turns and walks toward the front of the tent.

"Thanks. I was debating how to handle Ms. Parsons. I'm no Clint Eastwood."

"You're safe. Remember it was Chip Tyler she was after . . . Not you."

"What did I do with my beer? I know it was around here."

"If I didn't know better, you've either had one too many or are having a senior moment. Since I saw the Sheriff guzzle your first beer and saw that you didn't even have a sip of the second, I am attributing your misplaced beer to a senior moment."

"Gee thanks for being so supportive. I notice that you don't have your beer either. How do you explain that?"

"Your beer simply kidnapped my beer and now they are both on the lamb."

I stoke my chin in imitation of our esteemed leader. "Well reasoned . . . Well reasoned. My dear Watson, there's a simple solution . . . Get another beer."

"However, I think we had better pay a visit to the sleeping beauty without additional booze in hand."

"I guess everyone in the Sheriff's department is a party pooper."

Olivia hooks her arm with mine and we go off in search of the track manager's office . . . And the cougar therein.

CHAPTER TWENTY-THREE

The manager's office is easy to find and just far enough away from the festivities tent as not to arise any suspicion. Suspicion of what? I knock on the door. No reply. I knock again-somewhat louder. Again-no reply. I glance at Olivia in my *one eyebrow raised* look. "Now what?"

Olivia hesitates. I wonder if she is contemplating a search of her handbag for something with a bit of bang for the buck. Bad pun, but I am sure she is packing. Without further ado, Olivia grabs the knob to the office door and turns. The noise from within is terrifying. Stephanie Parsons is laying on large leather couch-clutching a blanket-and snoring as loud as any lumberjack I have ever met. I've never actually met a lumberjack, but I love the imagery.

"We know she's alive." Olivia is trying hard not to burst into gales of laughter. "I thought cougars growled." She loses it and starts to laugh. It's infectious. I join.

"Snort . . . Snort. Who's there? Is that you Josh?"

The otherwise staid Corporal Nederfield starts to shake her head. "No Ms. Parsons. It's Thomas and Olivia. Josh asked us to look in on you. He has had to go home . . . To his wife . . . And children." I have just had a lesson in how a woman can achieve a black belt in cattiness.

"He was so nice to help me try to find Charlie." Stephanie Parsons sounds like a Mack truck starting its engine. Cough-Cough-Sputter-Sputter. I have no doubt that she was really drunk. You just can't fake that sound. "Have you seen him?"

"Who?" Is she talking about Josh or Tyler?

"Why Charlie, of course. I need to talk to him. I found out some things about his *honey* that he should know. Do you know that LeMont is not her real name?"

We may be on a roll. Listen and say as little as possible-as difficult as that seems.

"Why no, we didn't" Olivia replies.

"Well let me tell you. She is a piece of work. The carnage she had left behind is amazing. I was initially very upset when he stopped seeing me after she had swept into his life. The more I thought about it, the more I realized that if *she* could make him happy . . . I could live with it." Ms. Parsons stifles a sniffle.

I wonder if although she *could live with* it, she possibly felt that Tyler couldn't.

"Fortunately the real estate market has improved and I was very busy with work. I'm divorced you know and my husband is a cheap S.O.B. So work I must and did. Then I heard about Monica . . . What's her name? And did I hear an ear full. Our Miss Monica was living as Mary Lewiston in Naples. She was literally run out of town. Tar and feathering is too good for her. I think she may have even had an altercation with the law. If you'll excuse me, I have to powder my nose." She rises and goes to the back of the office, knocks on a door of an obviously empty bathroom, enters and closes the door.

"Do you think there's a back entrance?" I whisper.

"You mean like a window she is going to climb out and disappear?" I guess Olivia doesn't think that is likely. She's probably right.

In about two minutes, Stephanie Parsons reappears. She has freshened up and seems raring to go.

"Now where was I? Oh yes . . . The . . . " She stops herself. "I am not going to lower myself to her level by name calling. In any event, I felt that it was my duty to tell Charlie that his girlfriend was not who she was trying to be. Actually, I really care for him . . . And she is even older than I am."

Whoa, now there's a *non sequitur.*

"I called Charlie several times last week, but he never returned my calls. I didn't say anything about *her*, only that it was important we talk. On Monday in the middle of the day, he called me at my office. He wanted *to talk to me about Monica*, he said. I hadn't said a word about her. I then said that I wanted to share some things about her, as well. He sounded very curious. He also sounded very hurt. I am quite attuned to his vibes. I said we could meet on Thursday afternoon in Palm Beach. He said *he had to go get his car ready for the weekend.* I asked him where he wanted to meet. He said *Wednesday morning.* As much as I wanted to meet him, I had a closing scheduled which I knew would take quite a lot of time. We settled on Friday, here at the track, around six. I wasn't sure what to expect. It would be too late to go back to Palm Beach that evening, so I got a room at the Hanging Moss Hotel at the airport . . . Just in case."

"In case of what?" I think it's a logical question.

"Well, I wasn't sure how our meeting was going to go and I wanted an option."

"Stephanie, I'm sorry, Thomas is a bit dense. I understand perfectly," Olivia says.

"Huh?"

"See what I mean?" The two women have a conspiratorial exchange.

"Did you two meet last night?"

"Yes. I arrived around 4:00. Traffic was a lot lighter than I had thought it would be, especially with the concert and everything. Anyway, I found Charlie's RV, but thought that I shouldn't arrive two hours early. Better fashionably late, than one minute too early. I decided to listen to some music and assemble my thoughts. I am ten years older than Charlie, which doesn't bother me, but could be a deterrent to a relationship. People might talk. You know. I can deal with it, but Charlie is so sensitive about what people say. Maybe that's why he acts so stupidly sometimes, so he can pretend he doesn't care what others are saying. He tries to be a bad boy and wants everyone to talk about his antics. But that's not really him. Being around his father without the benefit of a stable woman has made him act out. Then I thought that maybe my age would be an advantage to our relationship. Needless to say, I was vacillating. Then I thought about *Monica* and started to get angry. What a bitch . . . Oops . . . I mean she is trying make him believe she is his age!"

I am not sure how much more of this I can take. I may move away from the *Fatal Attraction* label and begin to think of other suspects. But since we are in for a dime, we might as well stay in for a dollar.

I am glad Corporal Nederfield takes over. "Stephanie, did you and Charlie meet at six?"

"Oh, yes . . . Sort of. Like I got to his RV and he was inside . . . Very upset. He kept on saying *someone was sabotaging his car so that it wouldn't work right and making him look bad.* Remember how Charlie really cares about what others think. Anyway he said *that his mechanic couldn't find anything wrong.* He was very frustrated. I tried to calm him down and asked if he wanted a shoulder message. He smiled in the way only he could. I also asked if he wanted a glass of wine. He said, *yes, that would be nice.* I had brought a bottle of Pinot Noir and two glasses with me. Charlie likes Pinot Noir."

She just used the present tense-*likes*-not *liked*. I don't think she has a clue about his murder, but I am not prepared to bet the farm just yet.

"I bought a screw-off top bottle so I wouldn't have to deal with an opener, but I brought some nice crystal glasses from home. Anyway, I think I was able to calm him down a bit, but he was still wound up about his car and said that he was *going to get to the bottom of the problem.* I asked him if he needed me to stay. He said that *he had a lot on his mind and wanted to be clear headed for the race tomorrow,* but he asked me if I would like to come to tonight's gathering. You bet! That's why I can't understand why he's not here. He really seemed to want me to be here."

I sure don't have the nerve to tell her. She would probably have a heart attack.

"I am sure one of us will find him. Why don't you check around and we'll do the same. By the way, did Charlie have any bad habits other than a glass of wine?""

"Funny, I asked him that about a year ago and he said he didn't like smoking anything, but I heard that the Monica creature was into drugs."

"Here is my card with my cell phone number. Call me if you find anything. We'll do the same." I hated lying to this lady, who will find the truth soon enough. "Are you okay?"

"Yes . . . And no, but I'll manage. Thank that nice man, Josh. I was in a very bad way. I'll call."

Olivia and I said our good-byes and left the office. We quickly moved away-in silence. "Do you have to do this sort of thing often?" I ask.

"Way too often," She answered. We both glanced back at the office and saw Stephanie Parsons leave.

"This sucks," I say.

"Yup. However, I think we can safely cross one person off our suspect list."

I raise an eyebrow.

CHAPTER TWENTY-FOUR

"I need that beer now."

"Me, too," Olivia responds.

"I need some time to ponder all the information we just got."

"Shit!"

"What?" I ask.

"I forgot to ask Stephanie what time she left the trailer."

"She got there at six and I think they drank the wine and she cleaned up the wine bottle and *crystal glasses from home*, and left. Makes sense?"

"I think the time line is crucial, so when she left is important." Olivia opens her pocket book and removes another folder. "Look at Tyler's phone log. Three calls between five and six yesterday; his Dad for ten minutes; Monica for almost forty minutes; and another short call to his father then no calls until about 7:20 p.m., which is presumably right after Stephanie left. Wait! That call is from Stephanie and it lasts about three minutes."

"Maybe she was calling to say she forgot something." That works for me-somewhat. "I think we should find Stephanie and ask her before she finds out what happened. I would love to see her cell phone log, but she might become very defensive if we ask. Also I want to know what Tyler was wearing. Did he change between her visit and his death?"

"At some point we will have to tell her that we are law enforcement," Olivia states.

"Yeh. And we should be the ones to tell her about Tyler. At least when she falls apart, there will be someone to provide some support," I say in agreement.

"Here's the other side, before we say anything about the murder, we have to eliminate her as a suspect." Corporal Nederfield is absolutely correct.

"Let's track her down before she disappears," I suggest.

"Suggestions?"

"The bar." I hope I don't sound mean, but after *tying one on*, Ms. Parsons is either going to need a stiff drink or a soft drink.

Since we were going for a beer anyway, we simply increase our pace.

"Success," I announce as we reach the refreshment line, in which Stephanie is just leaving.

"I'll cut her off," Olivia volunteers. "You get our beers." She smiles and glides toward the front of the line. "Stephanie, we meet again."

"My mouth feels like I swallowed cotton. I needed a Dr. Pepper."

Everyone seems to be into Dr. Pepper. I quickly secure our beers and join the ladies. After handling Olivia her glass, I say, "Cheers." I am not sure what we are cheering, but I want to put Ms. Parsons at ease before I say, "I forgot to ask you a couple of silly questions."

"The journalist's need for information, I assume," She replies after taking a long drink from her cup. "Fire away."

Since I figure I've got this last bite out of the information apple, I ask, "What time did you leave Charlie's RV last night?"

"A few minutes after 7:00. I remember glancing at my watch because I was getting hungry. I called Charlie's cell and asked him if he wanted to grab a bite to eat. He said *he wasn't hungry, but was looking forward to dinner . . . Tonight.* I told him that I was concerned about him. He laughed, but not with a lot of enthusiasm."

"Two more quick questions: what was Charlie wearing when you left and what happened to the wine bottle and glasses?"

"That's easy . . . I took the bottle and glasses with me. They were crystal glasses from home and matched my others. Charlie was wearing beige pants . . . Chinos. Freshly ironed. He had on brown loafers with tassels and a peach, almost coral, button down Oxford long sleeve shirt with the cuffs turned up. I thought he was simply scrumptious." She smiles at the thought. There is no way I am going to tell her about what happened-at least not now.

Olivia places her arm on Stephanie's. "I am sure that everything will work out. Thank you for all your help. Maybe you should go back to the hotel and get some rest. If anything happens, I'll call you. Do you have a card with your cell number?"

"I'd be a terrible real estate broker if I didn't." Stephanie removes a silver business card case from the pocket of her blazer, opens it and hands a card to Olivia and one to me. "I am a little tired. Maybe I will go back to my room and wait for Charlie to call. I'm sure he simply got tied up and lost track of the time." She gives Olivia a quick hug and walks toward the tent exit.

I take a large swallow of beer. So does Olivia.

"I think we can eliminate her as a suspect, don't you?" I pose to Corporal Nederfield.

"Unless she is a better actress than Meryl Streep, which I doubt, she is clearly off the list," she replies.

"Now what?"

"Finish our beer . . . Then find Josh. He has got to be home by 9 o'clock sharp and it's almost 8."

CHAPTER TWENTY-FIVE

"Which brings me to the next question, what do we have on the 3 M's: Monica, Mildred and Mary?"

"I am having her record run. Actually the rap sheet belonging to the fingerprints. We may turn up more *Monica's*. You know, I should have it by now. I'll need power up my tablet. My damn cell phone screen is too small." Olivia is on a roll.

"Do you think we should have asked Stephanie, what she had on Monica?"

"Although I never want to under estimate the effectiveness of the grape vine, she probably has a combination of fact and rumor and just plain *fake news*. I think we should limit ourselves to what we can find from sources we can use in court."

"Wow! You don't think much of Monica, do you?" I am a firm believer that women are possessed with a special skill set, which men call a *woman's intuition*.

"Thomas, there are a lot of unknowns and I don't want to speculate until we can put all three aliases together. Having said that, there is something about her that makes the hair on my arms stand up and tingle."

"Here's to intuition." I take a long sip of beer.

"Call it a well-honed instinct. From years of being called upon to make initial judgments based on few facts."

I hope this is not going to get me in trouble. "And how many of those initial judgments turn out to be correct?"

"Virtually every one." Olivia *clinks* her plastic cup to mine, raises it to her lips and drains the contents. "Virtually every one." She gives me a quick peck on the cheek. "Let's go find the super cop. I want to see who has gotten back to me and what he has uncovered in his travels."

The crowd is thinning as the food is waning and a 6'3" cop is easy to spot-so is the flamboyantly dressed *mouthpiece*, who is still holding court. Bad pun-again.

"I need you to share some of your intuition about pink pants," I say.

"If class was a measure of wealth, Attorney Bradshaw would have long ago been adjudicated bankrupt." Olivia has a way with words.

"I agree . . . But is he still a suspect?"

"Motive . . . Motive . . . Motive."

"I also agree, but what is he doing here?"

"Maybe he likes cars."

"Hardly the venue for an ambulance chaser."

Olivia strokes her chin. McCarthy is teaching us bad habits. "Thomas, there is something going on with Bradshaw, but whether it involves a homicide is clearly . . . Not clear."

"He is still on my list, if for no other reason; one does not wear pink pants to a race car event."

I can see that Olivia is trying to prevent herself from mirth and merriment. "If he goes to the concert, he can stay on our list." We both start laughing with enough gusto that several patrons turn around and Josh starts toward us.

"You guys are great under-cover investigators. Very inconspicuous."

"Just you wait until we disclose the amazing stuff we have learned . . . Under-cover." I resist thumbing my nose. "Seriously, we got a lot to go over. Let's go back to Maison Ballard and compare notes. Stephanie needs to check her email."

"And you have got to leave in about twenty minutes," Olivia inserts.

"One wife to nag me is all I want." I am waiting for Sheriff McCarthy to stamp his foot.

"Maybe all you want, but not all you need." I am taking my life in my hands.

"Let's go . . . Children," our den mother interjects. "There is really a lot we need to go over."

We scurry out of the tent and head to Paddock A and my awaiting abode. Olivia is right, we have actually learned a lot in the last hour, but I can't wait until the real Monica is unveiled. I wonder if she is still with Tyler the Elder or was she actually waiting for Tyler the Younger. Curious, more curious and most curious. I start to walk faster. Olivia and Josh have no trouble keeping up.

I reach into my pocket and remove a wad of keys. It's getting dark and I start fumbling around for the right key trick. Olivia shines her phone flashlight onto my hands. I easily find the key to the castle.

"Why don't you put a motion detector with a light over your door?" The Orange County Sheriff asks in an, *I know it all* kind of voice.

"When I get my check from your office for all my efforts on this case, I will invest in an alarm system. Maybe the kind that connects with my cell phone so that I can always see what's going on inside and out." I am feeling a little defensive.

"Gentlemen, have you listened to this dialogue?" We both stare down and shuffle our feet. "You are brilliant!" I am not sure where the Olivia is going, but I love the compliment.

"I never thought to check Tyler's RV to see if it has a security system and I was so busy checking phone numbers, I never examined his apps. I am going to call . . . "

"McCarthy here," Josh is almost shouting into his cell phone. "Get someone down to the RV that came in this morning with the dead guy in it. See if it has some kind of security system. Call Corporal Nederfield with what you find. Also, leave a message for Detective Rogers to call me first thing in the morning. He's on at 6. Thanks."

"As I was about to say, I am going to call and get someone to check out the RV, but I seem to have been too slow on the draw."

"Actions speak louder than words," Sheriff McCarthy proudly announces and gets a dirty glare from Olivia. "Only kidding. This has been a total team effort . . . But I'm the quarterback."

"The quarterback has about ten minutes to tell us what he found out so we can tell him about the enlightening conversation we had with Stephanie Parsons."

"Bottom line is that Emily Lange's presence at the race track has absolutely nothing to do with Tyler's death."

"Absolutely nothing?" I question the Sheriff's strength of conviction. "Her fingerprints are in the RV, she made a call to Tyler Friday and she was seen both last night and today."

"But there is a very good explanation," Josh replies.

"How good is very good?" Even Olivia is sounding a bit cynical.

"She is doing a piece on the race and concert for her TV station. She wants to get out of the weather lady mold and become a serious investigative reporter. Her superior at the station agreed to give her a chance and she has been here since Friday morning with a film crew, which has everything recorded." Sheriff McCarthy seems pleased with himself.

"Please explain the connection with Tyler." Corporal Nederfield wants to make sure the Chief hasn't let anything slip by.

"Simple. She was interviewing drivers, crews, spectators, band members . . . Like everybody she could think of. I guess they overshoot so that they have plenty of footage to edit. Since Charles William Tyler III was one of the younger drivers . . . And his father was one of the owner's of the track, Ms. Lange thought he would be a good candidate for an on-screen twenty seconds. Her assistant set it up last week and she called him Friday to confirm. She went to the RV at about 7:30 last night and spent about ten minutes with him. It's all on tape. Well, it's all digitally recorded with time coding. I saw it."

"Josh, what was Tyler wearing?" I ask.

"Wearing? Why?" He responds.

"We want to corroborate what Stephanie Parsons told us," Olivia answers.

"Let's see . . . Chinos and a button down shirt." Josh starts his chin rubbing routine.

"Color of shirt?" I ask.

"Kind of a light pinkish. Like peach."

"Bingo! Matches what he was wearing thirty minutes earlier."

"Is it important?"

"It might be," Olivia starts to explain. "It depends on what he was wearing when he was killed. Thomas?"

"You're right. Let me think. Beige pants for sure. The shirt was blood stained, but peach or coral color would be right."

"I'll make a note to call the coroner's office," Olivia offers. "Do either of you know what kind of shoes he was wearing?"

"The film showed him from about the waist up." Josh is still stroking his chin.

"I only saw the bottom because he was lying face down, but I would say his shoes were loafers. They weren't sneakers or sandals. They had leather bottoms." I nod, trying to convince myself that I have remembered everything.

"Boss?" Josh glances over at Olivia. "How did Tyler seem during the interview? Upset? Angry?"

"He was cocky. Very sure of himself. He did have a hard time after she asked him about having so many off track excursions during the day. Blamed it on a mechanical problem. He said something about his car wasn't braking properly. That was about the end of it. She said goodbye and wished him good luck. The camera followed her out of the RV. She then walked toward the concert entrance, followed by her faithful film crew. Well actually a guy with a camera and one with a sound boom."

"How did you get all this in less than thirty minutes?" I confess, I am very impressed.

"I guess my mug is on the TV more than I ever imagined. She said *good evening Sheriff* when I was almost ten feet away from her. The rest was just brilliant police work. I don't think she has any clue that young Tyler is dead."

I roll my eyes. But it seems like two suspects have been eliminated this evening.

"We were busy as well. With Ms. Parsons, who had pretty much slept off the hair of the dog by the time we returned to the manager's office." I peer over at Olivia, who picks up the tale of our conversations with the Palm Beach realtor.

"You need to say good-bye, Sir," Corporal Nederfield formally announces after she finishes. "There is nothing more we can do tonight. We need to contemplate what we have so far and wait for feedback from the medical examiner."

"We've got to wait for someone to examine the RV for security devices and his phone," I add.

"Okay . . . I'm out of here. Tomorrow at 9? Thomas? Corporal?" We both nod. "What kind of bagels do you like?" Josh asks with a smile.

"Whole grain!" Olivia and I answer simultaneously.

"That's easy. Don't get in any trouble tonight." Josh is having a real chuckle at our expense.

We stand and wave as he leaves. Olivia slips her hand into mine. "I need to freshen up before we go to the concert."

"Me, too." I sound moderately inarticulate.

CHAPTER TWENTY-SIX

I feel better having splashed a little water on my face, used a little deodorant and run a comb through my otherwise unruly hair. Olivia spent the same amount of time cleaning up as I did, but the results are dramatically different-she is radiant.

"Special Deputy Ballard, by virtue of my superior rank, I hereby declare this investigation closed for the night. I am not going to even open my tablet, since even if Monica is a serial murderer, escaped from a maximum security prison; there is nothing we will be able to do about it . . . Tonight. The less she suspects that we suspect, the easier it will be to get information from her directly."

"What about Clifford? You're right, he'll be here tomorrow and I am sure that either he saw Tyler the Elder or the other way around. Anyway I am on cranial overload."

"You poor baby," Olivia coos. "Let's go meet up with the Bentley folks and listen to some music."

This woman is something extraordinary. Then a little birdie says to me, *Remember Thomas, Olivia Nederfield is your colleague in the investigation of a murder, albeit a very cordial colleague.* Good point.

"I'm ready." I open the Airstream's door and offer my hand to help Olivia navigate the three stairs. Sir Walter Raleigh I am not, but at least I get to hold her hand. She alights, I close and lock the door and bow-ever so slightly.

"It's prince charming taking me to the ball. Well . . . Concert." Olivia hooks her arm in mine and pulls me closer to her. No complaints. Shoo, little birdie. "Do you think we'll need jackets?"

"It's still pretty warm, but it might be a good idea. It's Florida don't you know."

"I think I'll put up Vanessa's top."

"Don't want her to catch a cold." I get a punch in the arm. What did I expect?

"If she gets sick, I'll make you stay up all night with her." Olivia's smile radiates, even in the darkness.

"I'll help."

Two latches on the windshield and the canvas top is secure. "Let's roll up the windows. Keep the dew out." Vanessa is spoiled rotten. Olivia reaches into the back seat and takes out two lightweight nylon jackets and immediately tosses one back onto the seat. "I don't think a windbreaker with the word *SHERIFF* stenciled in bright yellow on the back would be well received at the concert." She wraps the jacket around her waist, wraps her arm around mine and says, "Okay, now I'm ready."

As quiet as the race track has become, the concert is reaching heretofore unknown decibels.

As we approach the entrance to the music venue, I notice that security guards are checking coolers and backpacks. In the old days they were searching for alcohol being smuggled in by underage kids, but now . . . I shudder at the thought.

"There they are," Olivia points to the Bentley gang.

I immediately start chuckling . . .

"Thomas . . . What is it?"

"Do you remember the children's book series, *Madeline*?" I ask.

"You are so spot on," Olivia replies.

By way of explanation, the members of the Bentley gang are lined up two by two with Margarite at the front. It's just like the covers on all the *Madeline* books; the children lined up behind Mother Superior. The imagery may not appeal to everyone, but clearly Olivia likes it. She is trying to walk and stifle a laugh at the same time. Tears are forming in the corners of her eyes.

"Thomas . . . Olivia!" Hans shouts. "We are waiting to go through the security check. A cruel reminder of the world in which we now live."

"We will see you right inside the gate. Privilege of the press." We wave.

Both Olivia and I show our shields and ID to the guard.

"Privilege of the press?" Olivia gives me a little nudge in the ribs.

"Stop beating on me," I retort.

She leaves over and gives me a kiss albeit on the cheek-again.

"All better?"

"Kind of." I can be a brat when I try.

The infield is packed with people; old people, young people, blue jean and plaid shirt people, tank top and cut off people and-I can't believe this-pink pants people-well actually a person. "Look who is here." I nod with my head in the direction of the bombastic barrister.

Before Olivia can answer, we are surrounded by our friends and a new band begins to play. The score board at the start/finish line is now a jumbo-tron with a twenty foot picture of the newest musical offering: City Lights-Country

Nights. The group plays a combination of traditional country and urban R and B-thus its name, which I think is very clever. The throngs in attendance are clearly enjoying the music. Folks are gyrating to the sound. They are not dancing, they are gyrating.

Olivia next to me and whispers, "What is Mr. Pink Pants doing here?"

"Super question. Let's keep an eye on him."

"Shouldn't be too hard to do. No one has ever called him *understated*."

"Shall we all have a beer?" The affable Welshman, Stanford, asks.

"Margarite, my dear, I do not expect them to have a drinkable wine, if they even have any at all," Hans suggests.

"Then I shall have a beer," She answers. Class act.

"My treat!" I offer.

"Nonsense," Hans says. "I know how much a journalist is compensated, and our merry group earns more per day than I trust you do in a year."

"Do not talk of such things, Hans. It is unseemly. Thomas, thank you for your offer, but these children have more money than they know what to do with and sharing a drink with new-found friends is a pleasure and a special treat. We actually know about you from your writing and yet you know nothing of us. Nevertheless, you extended us hospitality. Nothing more is to be said about the matter. Frederick would be so kind as to assist Stanford in getting the beer. We will be milling about in this locale, since there don't appear to be seats." Mother Superior has decreed.

"I apologize," Hans starts. "I spoke rudely. Please do not take offense. We have been together a long time. I let the moment get the best of me. Your gesture was genuine, my response . . . Asinine."

"It is already forgotten," I respond.

Olivia approaches Margarite and asks, "Do you like this type of music?"

"I think that American music has its roots in the culture of the people who immigrated here during several centuries. What I most appreciate is the lack of strict rules which otherwise limit the composer's or musician's ability to express him or herself. Classical music brings out the works' technical aspects more than being a reflection of the time and place when and where it was composed. American music, like your country, is free-spirited and adaptable. These young men and women performing on stage are merging different traditional styles and making something new. That is not done in classical performances."

"You have obviously thought about musical styles a great deal." I am very impressed by the succinctness of Margarite's observation.

"I have fortunately been given the opportunity to study music, art and literature my entire life." Margarite shrugs her shoulders in that very unique French way while during the palms of her hands upward. Her gesture says it all.

"Come on Frederick!" We hear Stanford shout. "These blokes will die of thirst if we don't get a move on it."

"Coming, you old nag." It's the first thing I've heard Frederick say. His voice resonates like cannon.

"Stop making fools of yourselves." Margarite puts her hand up, imitating a crossing guard, to slow down the two who are race walking while each carries a tray of beers. The men, each of whom is in his seventies, stop immediately. "That's better." Margarite removes a beer from Frederick's tray and hands it to Olivia and immediately turns, removes one from Stanford's tray and hands it to me. The two are standing as still as the soldiers in front of Buckingham palace.

Margarite then takes another beer from Frederick's tray, raises it toward Olivia and me and says, "May you stay on the path that will lead to truth." She sips; we follow, as Stanford and Frederick distribute the remaining beers.

I am really not sure how to interpret her toast. Margarite Leiter is so multi-faceted in so many ways. I hope she isn't a psychic and somehow knows that Olivia and I are seeking the truth. The truth about a murder.

The band begins another song, featuring a duet; an Afro-American man singing a bluesy baritone and an Asia woman singing a twangy Southern lower range soprano. The melding of their voices is amazing.

"See what I mean about the way American music is so adaptable," Margarite says. We are all glued to the images on the jumbo-tron and the sound coming from the scores of speakers through the venue.

CHAPTER TWENTY-SEVEN

I glance over to where I saw the audacious attorney when we entered. He's still there and still pink. Rather than watching the performance, he appears to be giving his business cards to several people who have gathered around him. I can't take him as a serious suspect because I can't tie him to Chip Tyler, but he must be guilty of something. Where are the fashion police when you need them most? I gaze back toward the huge screen. Olivia moves next to me and takes gentle hold of my hand. In a fit of insanity, I raise her hand and kiss it. I am awarded by yet another kiss on the cheek.

"You're very special," She whispers.

Rather than say something real stupid, I simply give her hand a brief, gentle squeeze.

The music seems to make everything alright. Thinking about finding a murder is definitely taking a back seat. Between numbers, the Bentley Boys plus one, which is what we now call our new friends, are absolutely charming, telling stories of their individual and collective exploits. The six men met over forty years ago at the University College in London as young engineering graduate students. They found they all liked the same things: travel, adventure and fast cars. They formed a company: Worldwide Exploration Consultants,

Limited, specializing in geosciences, which means mineral, gas and oil. They traveled all over the world providing advice to mostly third world countries on how to exploit their natural resources in an environmentally responsible and economically feasible manner. Margarite was married to Hans when they all met and she has been the stabilizing influence throughout several failed marriages, numerous car crashes, three riots, two boat sinkings and at least one civil war. Along the way, the Bentley Boys acquired quite a fleet of their namesake cars, many they have restored as museum pieces, many as vintage race cars and each drives as a regular daily vehicle the model he thinks is most emblematic of the marquee. They also acquired along the way-considerable fortunes.

They are very philanthropic, but one sees Margarite's hand in everything: creating and supporting a facility for retired musicians in Switzerland, sponsoring the expansion of three different childhood diabetes centers in France, England and the U.S., funding orphanages in Africa and Southeast Asia, and backing a world-wide study into the early diagnosis and treatment of different types of dementia, which she says is completely selfish because she hopes research will yield a cure before her *children* are inflicted.

They are the most amazing people I have ever met. There is not a subject upon which one or more does not have a strong opinion-backed by meticulous research. Once the discussions get started Pierre, Franco and Charles join Hans, Frederick and Stanford. However, whenever a song begins, Margarite simply raises her hand and whoever is speaking stops-often in mid-sentence. It is hysterical to watch. It is so natural and unassuming. It is simply the way things are done.

The hour is getting late and I am concerned about Olivia driving home, where ever that is, and getting back here by nine in the morning. Another band takes the stage. The announcer announces, *Ladies and gentlemen, boys and girls, let me present . . . Bermuda Bluegrass.*

Olivia leans over and whispers, "I love bluegrass music."

So much for leaving the concert. It doesn't present a problem for me. I only *live* about a hundred yards away.

The group consists of six players, each with a different stringed instrument: fiddle, banjo, mandolin, bass, acoustic guitar and a Dobro, which is a guitar with a built in resonator. Bluegrass goes back to the 18th century and early settlers from Ireland, Scotland and England. Instruments take turns playing the basic melody and then improvising, much like jazz, while the remaining instruments simply accompany. When the first player retires to accompaniment, another takes over and plays the melody. A bluegrass song never sounds the same twice-and these musicians are great.

Undaunted, between numbers, we are regaled by the adventures of the Bentley Boys. After consuming our first beer, Stanford secretly sneaks off for replacements. I am not sure how I will feel tomorrow, but I feel great now. I wrap my arm around Olivia's waist during one very moving ballad. She rests her head on my shoulder. This is about as good as it gets. Great music, great stories and great companionship.

"Boys, it's time to go. You have to drive exhibition laps tomorrow at nine. Can you two join us?" Margarite has everything well in hand. "We will be driving the track in the Bentleys wearing period racing costumes. Several others will be joining us. It's not racing, but it's quite amusing. Hans, did you bring the extra driver's frock and goggles. I think our journalists should get a flavor of what racing was like right after the Great War."

"Capital!" Shouts Stanford.

"Tres bon!" Adds Pierre.

"Olivia, Thomas, do take a spin around with us tomorrow morning," Hans insists.

I shift my eyes from Olivia, then to Margarite. "We can go, but only for a few laps. We've got an appointment at 9 and we can't be late. Well, too late."

"Non ce problema!" Franco says.

"That's settled. We will meet you at 9. Do you like coffee or tea?" Margarite asks.

"Coffee!" Olivia and I answer together.

"And croissant?"

"Oui. Merci," Olivia replies.

"Bonne nuit," She says as she ushers her *boys* from the concert."

We wave.

"I can't remember having so much fun," Olivia says.

"Same. I hate to be a wet blanket, but we've got a very early morning."

Olivia puts her fingers on my lips. "Shush. We will simply have to wake up early. That's all."

"We?" I sputter

"We . . . But you need to be on your best behavior. I don't want you to get the wrong impression."

"Boy Scout's honor." I raise up three fingers as I had been taught many, many years ago. I cross the fingers of my other hand behind my back.

CHAPTER TWENTY-EIGHT

"I think we should set the alarm for 6 o'clock. I want to see if we have both the medical examiner's animated recreation and Monica's rap sheet. I also think we should review the call log and reconcile it with what we learned from Ms. Parsons and Ms. Lange."

"How are we going to let Josh know that we'll be driving around the track?" I think that he might blow a fuse if he's here and we are not.

"It's after 11 so calling is out of the question. I'll text him in the morning and tell him that we are going over . . . Whatever," Olivia replies.

"I think we should view the crime scene from another vantage point . . . All in the name of the investigation."

"You mean as we race along the straightaway?"

"Exactly, Corporal Nederfield."

"You do have an alarm clock, don't you, Special Deputy Ballard?"

"I awake by the sun."

"I'll set the alarm on my phone." She punches me-again. But it doesn't hurt. Either she is hitting less hard or I am getting tougher. Go figure.

"About sleeping arrangements, I only have one bed," I sheepishly say.

"I noticed. Do you want the right side of the bed or the left side?"

"Is the middle an option?"

"I have a better idea."

I am afraid that I might have really fumbled the ball. "Yes?"

"I'll get ready for bed first and then pick my side. You get whatever is left over. Fair?"

"Imminently so," I answer. We are both trying to suppress a bad case of the giggles as we walk to my trailer, carefully skirting around RV's, campers and tagalongs, but none as elegant as the Airstream. It would be in bad form to wake up the occupants, who neither know about the death of Chip Tyler, nor apparently, care.

My cell phone vibrates. It's Josh. Actually it's a text from the Sheriff: *Make it 9:30, promised to take the kids to a friend's house-get murder animated recreation-we need time line-J.*

"Someone is smiling upon us, my dear." I hand Olivia my phone.

"Clean living and a pure heart." She gives me another cheek kiss, which as I have said before, is a lot better than a punch. I return the kiss. Maybe I should ask for the right side of the bed. Only kidding. Since it's only a double bed, picking sides is almost irrelevant. The Airstream was built long before slide outs became popular. What you see is what you get.

"Are you going to be okay without air conditioning?" I ask.

"Actually, I was going to ask if there is an extra blanket. It's getting a bit chilly."

I nod, instead of saying something stupid like *I'll keep you warm if you get too cold*. I am glad I have a certain amount of self control. I unlock the door to Maison Ballard. I breathe a deep sigh.

"What's wrong?" Olivia asks.

"Josh is right. I watch too many cop shows. I am fanaticizing that someone had broken into the trailer and ransacked it searching for the fruits of our investigation." I am going to drive myself nuts.

"First of all Special Deputy Ballard, whatever fruits we have are in my bag or we just learned tonight. Second, I don't think anyone really suspects that we are investigating a murder, except Freddy, who we agree he is not a problem. And thirdly, you should save your fanaticizing for something important." She smiles-I melt-and then open the door.

"There is nothing left to say," I mumble.

"Good. Then don't talk. Let's get ready for bed. 6 o'clock will arrive before we know it. Where's the other shopping bag I brought?"

"I put it in the bedroom," I answer.

"Bye." Olivia turns and walks toward the back of the Airstream. I decide to give her a little room to do her articles de toilette and leave the trailer, relock the door and head over to the communal bathroom. It also saves water.

"I'm back," I announce after I return.

"Brush your teeth and come to bed," a voice says from behind the bedroom door. It's Olivia's voice. Duh.

I lock up, turn off all the lights except a security light over the door, enter the bathroom, which smells better than it has ever smelled before and give my pearly whites a brisk brush. Being the gentleman my mother raised me to be, I contemplate what I should wear to bed. I opt for boxer shorts and a clean tee-shirt. I knock.

"Entrer."

I enter. Corporal Olivia Nederfield is lying on my bed, her blond hair cascading to her shoulders. This is no time to either have a stroke or to act dumb. I push the door partially closed so that a ray of light can be seen. I decide simple is best. I climb into bed, pull the sheet up to my chest, turn and give Olivia a kiss-on her cheek. She responds by giving me a kiss-on the lips-gentle and warm.

"Good night, Thomas."

"Sweet dreams, Olivia." We are asleep within a minute-holding hands under the blanket.

Heaven, I'm in heaven, and my heart beats so that I can hardly speak . . .

CHAPTER TWENTY-NINE

Dreams are funny things. They have been studied by countless numbers throughout the ages. Are dreams harbingers of things to be? Are they cruel reminders of things that have been? Are they visits of angry creatures from places far, far away? Or are they mechanisms by which we can escape the drudgery of day to day life?

I much prefer the school of thought that tells us that dreams are sweet respites allowing us to tip toe through the tulips in sublime peace.

"Get up lazy bones. I've already let you sleep an extra half hour."

Normally, being awakened in such a rude manner would put me in a foul mood, but since the voice is Olivia's, I'm okay with it. And the smell of freshly brewed coffee. Wait! What time is it? The concession stand doesn't open until 7.

The door to the bedroom is bumped open by a vision of loveliness-a tall, blond, wearing an oversized tee shirt and holding a steaming cup of java, the aroma from which tingles the brain into a state of semi-consciousness.

Rubbing my eyes, in part to wake up and in part to make sure I'm not still dreaming, I ask, "What time is it?"

"Exactly ten minutes after six. Up and at 'em. You get three sips of coffee, then off to the showers. I put a pair of clean jeans, a nice khaki colored safari shirt, clean drawers and socks on the table next to the door . . . And your shaving gear and towel from yesterday, which you should be glad you hung up since I can't find any others."

"When did you get up?" I am still a bit groggy.

"About a half hour ago. I've already had a shower, a cup of coffee and am ready to get dressed."

"Where did the coffee come from?"

"Thomas . . . My dear Thomas. I always carry zip lock bags of coffee, hot chocolate and sugar. All I need is hot water and it tastes like freshly brewed. Your propane stove works very well and you keep a very neat and tidy kitchen. Chop. Chop."

"Yes . . . Ma'am."

"Good."

"Good?"

"That you understand that I am in charge." Olivia slides over to the side of the bed and gives me a big, ole' kiss. For real on the lips. "Now get going. We've got a lot to do."

I swing out of bed, careful not to spill any coffee. "I'm off to the showers," I quip.

"Don't forget to wash behind your ears. I'll make the bed."

From anyone else, it might sound pushy, but from Olivia it sounds really good. I grab my gear, stuff my feet in shower shoes, an absolute necessity at any race track where they even pretend to have a shower, and sally forth. *It's going to be a warm one*, I say to myself as a blast of hot and humid air blasts me in the face. And it's not even 6:30. If I wasn't worried about waking those sleeping souls around my trailer, I might start to whistle-Zip-a-Dee- Doo-Dah. *My, oh, my, what a wonderful day.* Maybe I should opt for a cold shower. Nah. Feeling good is-good. And a hot shower feels good.

In an abundance of caution, I knock before entering my trailer.

"You may enter Sir Galahad. I have taken the liberty to freshen up your coffee," Olivia says once gain handing me a hot cup of coffee.

You may take liberties with me any time you wish, I say to myself, rather than sounding like an idiot. "Thanks. The coffee is great and much needed."

"I'm booting up my notebook. I want to see who has gotten back to me."

"May I have the call log? That can be our baseline." I think we are going to need more space than my petite dinette affords. "From Thursday morning until his death you said there were 22 calls, of which three were calls received, but which went into voice mail."

"Let's deal with the calls that we can use to corroborate witness statements. Stephanie Parsons call Tyler at 7:18 Friday, right after she left. That matches up. Her earlier calls are not on the call log, but I am sure we can retrieve them. Eliminate a call from his dentist, that's twenty calls. Emily Lange's call is consistent with her statement to us. Nineteen."

"What about Tyler's call to Bradshaw? How long was the call?" I am hoping that pink pants is somehow involved. I have always taken a dislike to him, although I have never met him. That's pretty petty, but nobody's perfect.

"About fifteen minute call at 11:23 Friday morning," Olivia responds.

"Another tidbit for our timetable." I hand Olivia the race schedule for the event. "Tyler was on the track from 9:45 to 10:15 for a practice session. He did something to his car and

Freddie had to fix it so that it could be re-inspected, which is when I met him yesterday morning."

"Meaning?"

"I'm not sure, but somehow Bradshaw is involved."

"Okay, but for purposes of attaching names to times, let's simply circle that call. That leaves us with eighteen calls. None to or from Clifford, fifteen to or from either Tyler's father or Miss Monica, and three unknown."

"Can we track down the unknown?' I ask.

"Since yesterday, I have been trying. Smaller cell providers are a problem. Their record retrieving capacity is limited on weekends. If the phone numbers are associated with an internet service, it is even more difficult. All three unknown numbers are associated with calls made to Tyler at these times." I lean over Olivia's shoulder to stare at the paperwork spread out on the table. She smells great. "We need to track down this 8:13 a.m. call to Tyler's phone; this 12:02 call Friday afternoon and this 5:17 call later in the afternoon."

"Could any of these unknown numbers be associated with Clifford?" I ask. "Wait! I have the answer." I search my call log for Bill Clifford's number. I place my phone next to the three mystery numbers. "Nope."

"Maybe." Corporal Nederfield has something on her mind. "Since we can't trace these numbers yet, they could still be in some way connected to anyone, including Clifford, although I admit, most people don't have two cell phones."

"Yeh, but most people don't stab someone in the back," I astutely observe.

"Very true, but lest we digress, we have fifteen calls involving Tyler the Elder and the mysterious Monica. Two are voice messages from the old man. Of the remaining, seven are to or from Monica's cell; three are to Mr. Tyler's office in Palm Beach and the remaining three are either to or from Mr. Tyler's cell."

"Olivia Nederfield, you are being very circumspect and I think I know why. We have observed that every time Monica appears, Mr. Tyler is by her side. Freddie alluded to it with a certain level of discomfort. We've seen it. So am I correct in concluding that for purposes of our timeline, we are not separating the two?"

"You are a very wise man, special deputy and you are quite stunning in your safari shirt. And ready for all things: a hunt for a wild animal or a cruise around the scene of the crime in an antique Bentley."

"And while we are on the subject, may I say you are ravishing in your green and beige sweater."

"British racing green to be precise."

How did she know we were going to a ride in an old English car when she packed her bag? And, by the way, how did she know to pack a bag?

CHAPTER THIRTY

"Unbelievable!" Olivia shouts as she opens the first of several emails from her office. "Monica, Mary and Mildred have quite the interesting legal interface history. About twenty years ago Mary Lewiston pleaded *no lo* to a charge of unauthorized use of a motor vehicle in Collier County. Ms. Lewiston received a 30 days sentence, which was suspended. Thereafter, Ms. Lewiston was very busy indeed. She was charged six times for insurance and/or check fraud and once for counterfeiting, and get this; the charges were dropped each time for lack of prosecution. She was born Mildred Letterbaum in Ames, Iowa and is 53 years old. She graduated from Central High School and Iowa State, majoring in business. After graduation she moved to Naples and changed her name to Mary Lewiston."

"Can you blame her with a name like Mildred Letterbaum?" I quip.

"But wait, there's more. About two years ago, she moved cross state from Naples to Palm Beach and changed her name . . . Again. This time she chose to be known as Monica LeMont. She has a Florida driver's license, a new Toyota Corolla and a mid six digit money market account at The Sunshine State Institute for Savings. Her current address is on Golf View Road in Palm Beach. Very upscale neighborhood."

"She certainly has done well for herself," I snidely say. I can't help myself. Our suspect list has been narrowed, but the motive remains elusive. "I'd like to get a better handle on her actual offenses like when, where and who."

"For what it's worth the charges seem to have been brought about every three years. Here's something interesting." Olivia pushes her computer toward me so that it is easier to read. "See the number 1-117? That means the offense is against a senior, which is defined in Florida as someone over 65."

"Basically, Chip Tyler's young, sweet girlfriend is neither young nor sweet. What was she doing with him? He seems all wrong for her *modus operandi*." I am trying to get a handle on Monica's scheme.

"If you were as much of a cynic as I am, you might say that she was using young Tyler to get to old Tyler." Corporal Nederfield is being really cynical, but there is more than a grain of truth in what she is saying.

"Olivia, what's the motive?" I ask.

"Knock off the kid so you can console the old man," she replies.

"That's a stretch."

"True, but stranger things are going on in this case."

"Let me ponder."

"While I contemplate."

"Sounds dirty."

"Only to you, Special Deputy Ballard. Let's go over the report from the medical examiner."

"Movie time?"

"No. Apparently the animation may take a bit longer. Something about the position of the body on the bed.

Thomas, what do you recall about Tyler's bedroom when you saw him and where was the body . . . Exactly?"

I close my eyes in an effort to concentrate on each detail. "No way!"

"What?"

"I see what's wrong. When I arrived Tyler's body was pretty much in the center of the bed, which I might add is considerably wider than mine . . . Ours. My initial reaction was that he had been stabbed while he was sleeping. There was a lot of blood near the wound in his back, but now I recall seeing some blood at the foot of the bed. And here's something else. He was wearing only one shoe. Where's the second shoe? We need to see the pictures the forensic people took at the crime scene."

"Let me take a quantum leap on this scenario. Tyler was stabbed while he was standing and fell onto the bed. To make it appear that he was killed while in bed, the murderer moved the body just a bit."

"If your, not so off the wall, theory is correct, Tyler's other shoe would be on the floor next to the bed, right?"

"Exactly. That would change the dynamics of the murder, including the angle of entry of the knife."

"Wouldn't it require someone very strong to move the body from the foot of the bed into the middle? So here's a variation of your theory to consider. Tyler was stabbed while standing. I am not sure whether he had been facing the assailant and turned, or had his back toward the assailant, but he fell onto the foot of the bed. Maybe after taking a couple of steps. I'm not sure whether the wound would initially bleed profusely enough for there to be blood on the floor. At some time shortly thereafter, Tyler had another visitor, who found the body and moved it."

"Too many bad TV shows. Why would the second person move Tyler?"

"Killer tells accomplice that young Tyler has been stabbed. Accomplice wants to cover up for killer and does some murder scene rearranging. Possibly to create an alibi for actual killer."

"I have a problem with conspiracies. We need to figure out if Tyler's murder was premeditated or spontaneous." Olivia starts to stroke her chin. I still think she has been hanging around Josh too long.

"I'm getting a headache," I announce.

"Me, too. We've identified nine sets of fingerprints in the RV. Monica might be the killer. I don't think the elder Tyler would kill his son, but he might move a body. My thoughts about Clifford are still up in the air. Stephanie Parson, Emily Lange and Freddie are all out . . . Pretty much. Bradshaw is an enigma. What is he doing at the track? I think that it is fair certain that we totally and unequivocally eliminate both you and the victim as suspects."

"Why thank you. Lest we forget, there are some heretofore not identified prints and three phone calls which we cannot trace."

"I would ask you for an ibuprofen but it doesn't do well on an empty stomach." Olivia is no longer stroking her chin, but is now rubbing her forehead.

"It's almost 8:30. I think we should take a slow walk over to the top of the main straightaway and join up with the Bentley boys . . . And girl. We need some fresh air and I want to stop at the bathroom. Two cups of coffee and nature calls."

Olivia smiles. "You make me laugh."

"Well in that case, I can do my Groucho Marx routine."

"That's okay. I'll pass . . . But not before I get another kiss."

I oblige.

144

CHAPTER THIRTY-ONE

The air feels a little less humid than it did earlier this morning. The evening's dampness is burning off under the warming Florida sun and is being replaced with some big puffy white clouds, which often change to dark gray by mid afternoon in advance of a typical thunderstorm, which stops as quickly as it starts. Olivia seems to be in less of a funk. I wouldn't want a daily diet of murder-solving. Not only is it bad for the health of the victim, the good guys have a lot of responsibility; often little to go on and a very narrow window of opportunity to solve the case before it gets cold.

Because it is Sunday, neither the music nor the race cars can be started until noon, which makes our stroll all the more pleasant. In order to keep the thousands of spectators at peak sensory overload, the event organizers have put together exhibition events featuring classic cars from the 20's and 30's-the golden age of automobiles. People can view these beauties up close and personal, while the lucky ones, like us, get to drive around the track pretending to be movie stars like Clark Gable and Katharine Hepburn, Rita Hayworth and Gary Cooper, of course, Bogie and Bacall.

Walking hand in hand with Corporal Olivia Nederfield almost forces me to say, *Hey kid, where've you been all my life?* I resist.

"Our time table is troubling me," I begin. "For starters, we are making assumptions inconsistent with certain facts."

"Explain Sherlock."

"Where people were at 7 or 8 o'clock Friday evening is basically irrelevant. We've been asking the wrong questions. Where were the members of our cast of characters when Tyler was stabbed, which is somewhere around midnight and say 3 in the morning? We need to check the report to see if the time of death can be narrowed somewhat."

"So basically, none of the suspects is really in the clear."

"Not unless they have an alibi that is ironclad. We have pretty much eliminated Stephanie Parsons and Emily Lange, although we really don't know where they were at the time of the murder."

"Back to square one?"

"Not necessarily. I've got an idea. Our Palm Beach realtor talked her way out of our investigation. As calm, cool and collected as she sounded, she has a motive. Where did she say she was staying?"

"Hanging Moss Hotel at the airport," Olivia answers.

"Bet they have surveillance cameras."

"Probably. I am not sure I am completely following you."

"If the cameras have Ms. Parsons entering the hotel at about 8 o'clock on Friday, her story is corroborated. Right?" I ask.

"Yeh, but I still don't see where you are going."

"What if the surveillance cameras also show her leaving the hotel around midnight?"

"Bingo!"

I take my cell phone from my pocket and start dialing. "Josh, sorry to bother you, but after you drop off the kids and before you come over to the track, I have an errand for you." I pause to listen to his response, which is relatively calm.

"Stephanie Parsons may have sold us all a bill of goods. Maybe not. But there is a way to find out. She is staying at the Hanging Moss Hotel at the airport. Being that you are the Sheriff of Orange County, I am sure that you can view their security tapes from 7:30 Friday evening to about 2 in the morning to see if Ms. Parsons came or went." I pause again.

"I know I am brilliant, but I still don't want your job. TTFN." I disconnect the call.

"TTFN?"

"It's how we have said good-bye since we were kids. TTFN . . . Ta ta for now.

"Oh brilliant one, how are we going to check Emily Lange's alibi."

"Not yet sure, but I am definitely less concerned about her. No motive."

"Well, if we see her I am going to ask her straight out." Corporal Nederfield has a bee in her proverbial bonnet. I really can't blame her since we seem to be going backwards. The slippery slope of crime solving.

"Let's meet up with our new friends. I'm looking forward to riding on the track."

"Me, too, and I'm starving. I'll bet Margarite is very fussy about her croissants."

Once again we start to walk toward the gathering gaggle of magnificent motorcars from a much simpler era. "These cars remind me of the time when men were men and women knew their place." I fully expect to be punched in the arm-rather hard.

"Ah yes. When men went out to work early each morning and came back late for supper and handed the little lady their paycheck."

"Touché!"

Olivia takes my hand and starts to quick march. "Come on slow poke. I see the Bentleys over there." She points to three of the huge green and black cars. They epitomize the definition of a *Town Car*, since an entire town can fit inside.

"Bonjour!" Hans waves.

Since I can't walk any faster, I simply return the wave and say, "Good morning." We are moving into a time warp, surrounded by moving pieces of art-the daring Duesenberg, the regal Rolls, the beautiful Bugatti and the alluring Allard. I am running out of adjectives for these fantastic cars. Whenever I am in the presence of so many classic cars, I start to create a kind of dialogue between them. The snappy Packard roadster asks the Delahaye cabriolet, *Seen any good movie . . . Stars lately?*

"Thomas, are you alright?" Olivia asks.

"Yes, of course. Why?"

"You were chuckling to yourself a minute ago."

"A chuckle a day, keeps the doctor away."

"You are crazy," Olivia observes.

"Over you, my dear. Over you." At least I don't get punched.

"You definitely need something to eat. Your brain is clearly weakened with hunger."

"Glad you could make it," Stanford says. "Coffee?"

"Wonderful. Two black cups is just what the doctor ordered." Olivia gives my hand a squeeze. Firm, but not too hard. I give her a kiss. Not too wet.

"Hans, how nice to be young," Margarite says. Hans give her a kiss on both cheers.

"Oui, mon cheri."

Margarite playfully slaps Hans' arm.

"Welcome, mes amies. Welcome."

CHAPTER THIRTY-TWO

Stanford and his side-kick Frederick rush up to us each holding a piping hot mug of coffee-in real ceramic mugs. Makes you hate Styrofoam. The mugs are-you guessed it-British Racing Green and feature a beige-colored stylized *B*. The color matches Olivia's sweater exactly. How could she possibly know?

"Come get some especiales de maison," Stanford says. He offers Olivia his arm to escort her. Frederick and I follow.

The three Bentleys form a large triangle, inside of which is the apotheosis of tailgating, the new standard by which I will hereafter judge all tailgates. Two linen clothed tables are adorned with silver service, including a candelabra, not lighted because of the proximity of so many classic British cars, with often leaking SU carburetors. I slowly absorb the perfection of the presentation. Not only do I spy said afore mentioned croissants, but dozens of other fruit topped pastries, together with small individual-portioned jars of jams, jellies and marmalades. Coffee is being served from an urn which sits next to an equally ornate samovar for hot water.

"Mademoiselle, monsieur, may I serve you something to eat?" Pierre asks.

"Merci," Olivia answers.

It is obvious that each member of the group has a specific assignment: Hans is the meeter and greeter; Stanford, with able assistance from Frederick, is responsible for beverages; Pierre is all about food; and Franco and Charles, who with quiet efficiency are checking over the cars, are the mechanics. Obviously, Margarite is majordomo. Hey, it all works.

"My darling, try a croissant with a soupcon of raspberry jam." I offer Olivia a plate.

"Darling? I guess it works for me . . . So long as the Sheriff is not around."

"You mean the ogre?"

"Yup."

"Will I have to turn in my special deputy badge if I want to take you to out to dine?"

"Only if I accept."

"You cut to the quick, fair damsel."

"You haven't extended the invitation and furthermore, we have a job to do." Olivia leans over and gives me a cheek kiss. I don't blush-much.

"No! No! No! It is done so" We all turn to face Margarite, who puts her hands gently upon my face and kisses me on one cheek and then another. "Now try it again."

It's Olivia's turn to blush, but she follows Margarite's order.

Suddenly I hear clapping-then *Bravo*, *Well done* and *I am available if you need to practice*, whereupon Margarite gives Stanford a gentle slap on the wrist.

"Enough! We need to eat. Franco . . . Charles, I am sure the tire pressure is perfect. Come have some food."

"Oui Madam," They reply in unison.

There is something really special about these folks. They have found peace with and amongst themselves.

"Thomas, I recall that you were about to offer me a croissant." I sincerely believe that Olivia's smile could light up a dark room.

"And abracadabra." I produce the previously proffered plate.

"Yum," Olivia says after taking a rather large bite. Since I gave her the plate, she probably thinks I meant she could eat the whole croissant. I'm cool with it.

"Let's check out the bountiful spread," I suggest.

Corporal Nederfield stuffs the remaining croissant into her mouth and mumbles something like, "Good plan."

Decisions, decisions. I think I shall have one of each, but reluctantly settle for a cherry tart AND a croissant with butter and orange marmalade-and another mug of coffee. Olivia chooses a slice of apple strudel AND a mille-feuille (a Napoleon).

"Beats the heck out of stale donuts and gas station coffee," I quip.

"I think I am about to burst," Olivia answers, after she swallows her final bite.

"I wonder where Margarite got all this?"

"I hope not in Orlando."

"Why?"

"Because I would weigh 200 pounds."

"No self control?" I smirk.

"Depends on what I am trying to control."

"Ouch. That hurts."

Margarite claps her hands. "Stanford and Franco into the Speed Six. Charles, Frederick, Thomas and Olivia into the 4 ½ liter. Hans and Pierre will take the Red Label. I will stay here and clean up."

"But, Cheri!" Hans exclaims.

"No buts. You've got to get the babies over to the start/finish line."

Everybody does as ordered-with good cheer.

Frederick opens the rear door of the giant four seat touring car and hands us ankle- length coats, and goggles. Early Bentleys were sold without bodies. The coachwork was done by custom shops like H. J. Mulliner, Thrupp & Maberly and Gurney Nutting. Our steed is a 1929 open tourer by Vanden Plas. It roars to life with Charles at the wheel-located on the right side of the car. I guess that fixing the car allows you to drive it. Franco is steering the Speed Six and Hans the Red Label. The sound is deafening in a pleasant sort of way. You know you are a part of history. Who else has been seated in the back seat of this dazzling auto?

Together with about forty other classics, we make our way to the start/finish line and stop.

"Thomas." Olivia lightly jabs my ribs with her elbow.

"At least we know that if Clifford is the murderer, he doesn't think he's a suspect," I suggest.

"Or he is trying to dazzle us with his convincing act of confidence."

"Not so convincing. Remember he was in my trailer around 12:30, which is clearly within the window during which the crime was committed. And he was the one who suggested I visit young Tyler in the morning." I am finding it harder to call him by name and easier to adopt the indifference of *victim* or *decedent*.

"At least we know he'll be around to interrogate later today." Corporal Nederfield's use of the word *interrogate* rather than *chat with* or *interview* is interesting. I think he is still high on her suspect list. I know he is on mine.

I must admit, Bill Clifford is all business-chief steward business. He announces through a microphone that the cars are the stars and this is simply an exhibition. No passing will be permitted unless a driver waves to the vehicle behind him to overtake his car. I peruse the spectator area. Despite the early hour on Sunday, thousands of fans are gathered everywhere. Car people and concert people.

The PA system crackles to life. *"Ladies and gentleman, I take great personal pleasure in announcing the Grand Marshall for our event. He will lead these marvelous machines around this fantastic facility in a 1914 Stutz Bearcat. From the world of auto racing **and** the world of Country and Western music, Ricky Nickerson, the only person to be in both the NASCAR Hall of Fame and the Country Music Hall of Fame."*

The thunderous applause that follows is richly deserved. I have had the opportunity to meet with Ricky Nickerson on several occasions and he is the real deal-a racing cowboy with a heart of gold and a wallet to back it up. He serves on the board of directors of numerous foundations, all of which benefit children. Even at over 80 years old, he still travels to events to raise money for his causes.

I join in the clapping, which might have continued forever, but for Ricky raising his hand to silence the crowd. He has a wireless microphone into which he says, *"Thank you all for that reception. I am simply a private in an army of thousands who battle against disease, poverty and bigotry. This weekend is to celebrate machines and music. But I want to pay special thanks to a group who has raised millions for our programs. I've had the pleasure to know these folks for over thirty years. I simply call them-the gang-and they are here today in those three beautiful Bentleys. Margarite, Hans, Stanford, Franco, Pierre, Frederick and Charles. True benefactors and true friends. Please stand up."*

The crowd, if possible, is even louder than before. Slowly the six men rise from their seats and wave.

"*Where's Margarite?*" Ricky asks.

The six turn in drill team precision and point up the track toward the place where we had our tailgate. There, standing alone, is Margarite, who places both hands on her mouth and blows a kiss to all.

"I am overwhelmed," Olivia whispers.

"Totally." Not very poetic, but it is all I can think of.

On with the show, the public address announcer says.

Simultaneously, four, six, eight, twelve and sixteen cylinder cars burst into life. I see a group of spectators standing along pit road. If I was wearing dentures, they would have dropped from my mouth. "Olivia," I whisper.

Her eyes follow mine. Standing in a small group is Charles William Tyler, Jr., Monica or whoever she is, and Attorney Bradshaw, who is now wearing a pair of garish lime green pants and a shiny black collared shirt with white buttons. Hideous. The three are being interviewed by Emily Lange. Her camera man and boom operator follow her like puppy dogs.

"This makes talking to the suspects easier. They are all here," observes Olivia.

"All but one," I respond.

"Ah yes. Ms. Parsons. I am really curious about what is on the security video. I wonder if she is planning on coming to the track."

I pull out my phone; search my call list and text the following: *Stephanie, we have some important information about Charlie. Can you come to the track around 11? Thomas and Olivia.* I show the message to Olivia who gives me thumbs up. I push the **SEND** button. I sit back in my seat as the Bentley gains speed and put my arm around Olivia' shoulders. She snuggles next to me. I glance at the speedometer and it indicates 70 miles per hour-and that's going through a corner. Other than the throaty sound of the exhaust, an occasional squeal of the tires and the wind blowing in our faces, it is hard to realize that we are riding in a car that is almost ninety years old.

Lap after lap we tour the track at a rather brisk rate of speed. Since we were gridded right behind Ricky Nickerson in the Stutz, we are putting down some rather hot laps. I peer over my shoulder and see the other two Bentleys close behind. Stanford gives us a wave. I'm glad Franco is driving. Despite the solid feel of the car, I suspect that two hands on the wheel is pretty much a pre-requisite. As a kid I loved to look at pictures of early automobile races. I mean racing before the First World War, when both a driver and a riding mechanic were required to literally throw the monsters around the track, slow them down and make sure the engine was properly lubricated. A lot of progress was made in twenty years. I lean over and give Olivia a kiss on the cheek. This is becoming a habit to which I could become accustomed.

CHAPTER THIRTY-THREE

I am quickly brought back to reality when my pocket starts to vibrate. Olivia feels it too. I retrieve the interloper from my pocket. "A text from Stephanie Parsons," I announce. "She's fine with 11 o'clock, but wants to know where to meet us."

"How about under the timing and scoring tower near the start/finish line?"

I nod and text the information. "Hail, hail, the gang's all here."

"Or will be. I hope the great one will be able to get the surveillance footage."

The car begins to slow. I look at my watch. We've been cruising around the track for over thirty minutes. "I don't want to go in yet."

"Back to work Special Deputy First Class Ballard."

"Do you outrank me?"

"You can count on it." She can be so mean.

The Bentleys glide back to the paddock where Margarite has not only cleaned up after breakfast, but has put leftovers in a bag for us. "The day is long and you will need to keep up your strength," she says.

"Our strength?" We ask together.

"For your investigation and I wish you good luck. Killing is such a nasty thing."

"Margarite, what do you know about an investigation?" I am clearly rattled.

"It is fine Thomas. The boys and I know what happened. I think you three have done an excellent job of keeping the matter discreetly quiet. I wish we could add to your pool of information, but alas, we know nothing about either why such a heinous occurrence took place or who might have committed the crime."

"Margarite," Olivia begins. "Without sounding . . . Harsh, how do you know anything about what happened?"

"My dear girl, please don't be upset. Very little escapes our eyes and ears. Do not worry. If we see or hear anything, we will find you. Au Revoir. I know you have much to do." Margarite hands Olivia the bag of leftovers. "Bonne chance."

I am dumbfounded. Somehow I gather enough presence of mind to say, "Thank you for . . . Everything. A bientot." I kiss her on both cheeks, turn, put my arm around Olivia's waist and begin to walk back to my trailer.

"Surreal. I have no other word for it. Surreal."

"I think we have been in the *Twilight Zone* for the last hour." I stop and turn to Olivia. "But it certainly has been interesting."

"There are so many things that I can't explain. Do you realize that the chances of all the major suspects still being around a day and a half after the murder are infinitely remote? But it has happened. And then there's the Bentley seven, who are beyond description." Corporal Nederfield is clearly without words.

"We've got to come up with a strategy. Subject to Josh's approval, I think we need to find Emily Lange and have another chat with her. She was observed by one of Freddie's guys around 11. She wasn't filming. It appeared that she was waiting for someone. Could that someone have been Chip Tyler?" I doubt many of our questions will ever get answered.

"I hope the security tapes show something regarding Ms. Parsons' whereabouts between 7:30 and a little after midnight Friday night. Thomas, what time is it?"

I stare at my trusty Rolex knockoff. "It's almost ten. We'd better hot foot it back to the trailer."

As we come around the back of my home away from home, Josh comes around the front, with a bag from Myers' Bagels. I wiggle my bag at him. He gives me one of those, *what are you trying to say Thomas?* type looks.

"I've got the bagels I said I'd bring, what do you have?"

"It's a long story, but those nice folks with the old Bentleys invited us to a tailgate this morning and we brought back a doggie bag."

"We?"

"It's not what you think," I sputter. "Or is it?" I give Olivia my best smile.

"Even if it is what you think, we have gotten a lot done." Corporal Nederfield has taken the wind out of the sails of the Sheriff of Orange County. "And we need to go over a lot of material before 11 o'clock."

"What's at 11?" Josh asks.

"Stephanie Parsons is meeting us," I answer.

"In addition to bringing food, I have a DVD of the images from six different cameras at the Hanging Moss Hotel. I haven't reviewed at them. After you called this morning, I thought I could reach out to the manager and give him a *head's up*. Good thing. Their security is not handled in-house but by an outside firm . . . Steinmetz Security."

"You mean like Richie?"

"The very same." Josh smiles.

"What are you two talking about?" Olivia feels left out.

"The guy who owns the security firm went to both elementary school and high school with us. He was a bit of a nerd, but once you got to know him, he was very funny . . . And very smart. His firm is one of the largest private security firms in Florida. They use state-of-the-art everything, much of which has been designed by Richie, who also licenses it to other firms."

"He does sound smart. Is he single?" I give Olivia one of those glares. "Only kidding," She says.

"So many zings, so early in the relationship." The Sheriff adds his two cents worth.

Corporal Olivia Nederfield turns to face me, places her hands on my cheeks and gives me a juicy kiss. "Such a fragile ego."

Josh shakes his head and says, "Excuse me, but we have a killer to catch and I have given up a Sunday with the family to do so." We both are like school children who have been reprimanded by the teacher. "As I was saying, when I found out that Richie's company did the surveillance, I called him at home. It turns out that the images are not recorded on premises, but transmitted to his office in Lake Nancy. He said he'd make a call and have the data copied onto a disc, which he offered to have delivered to the Registration building here at the track, where I picked it up ten minutes ago."

Now it's my turn. "The old boy's club has come through again." I can sense the hair on the back of Olivia's neck bristling, but she says nothing. I may pay for the remark later. At least I hope so.

"Sheriff McCarthy, may I have the disc and I will load it into my machine. The screen is a bit small for the three of us so I suggest Special Deputy First Class Ballard watch the video . . . Alone, while we go over the report from the coroner and the time line. I want to be able to either eliminate Ms. Parsons or put her back on the suspect list before she gets here."

When I said I may have to pay for my remark later, I didn't think *later* would be here in less than a minute. Actually, what she said is logical-more or less. I take the computer and retire to my bedroom where I prop myself up with a pillow and push **PLAY**. Once you get the hang of it, viewing the images from the six cameras in sequence is less difficult than I had thought. You get into a pattern, especially when you know what you are searching for or more precisely, who you are searching for. The frames are coded by date, time and camera location. I decide to take a shortcut and examine only images from the two cameras in the garage on the assumption that Stephanie Parsons would rather put her car in a lighted garage than park in a dark outside lot. However, I immediately encounter a minor glitch. I don't know what kind of car she drives. Shall I shout to the other room or get out of my comfy bed and inquire? I select the latter. I may have pushed a sensitive button with my *old boy's club* comment.

Josh and Olivia are reading the report on Tyler's death from her cell phone. "Would it be easier if you use my lap top with a 15 inch screen?" I ask.

"You never said you had a lap top," Olivia retorts.

"You never asked and furthermore I thought that it would occur to you that as a journalist, I am occasionally required to write articles and even post them on client websites."

"Children! Quiet!" Josh slams his hand onto the table. "Enough. We have work to do. Thomas your *old boy's club* remark was insensitive and Corporal, you are being just a bit too testy. So kiss and make up. And that's an order."

Olivia and I gaze at each other, roll our eyes and then kiss.

"I'm sorry. I need to think about what I am going to say before I say it." I can eat humble pie with the best of them. I open a drawer under the table and pull out my lap top. "It's fully charged and ready to go."

"You can be really sweet." Olivia gently touched my hand.

"I'm going to throw up if this keeps up." Sheriff McCarthy is an incurable romantic.

"What I came out to ask you is what kind of car does Ms. Parsons drive?"

"I have it right here. She drives a 2016 Lexus ES 350, silver, 4-door, Florida registration PBY P17."

"Perfect. Cheerio."

"Cheerio?" The Sheriff is baffled.

"We'll explain latter," Olivia offers. "Back to work. TTFN."

Josh and I explode with laughter.

CHAPTER THIRTY-FOUR

After twenty minutes, I start to feel a migraine invading my head. Throb. Throb. Throb. However, if I complain, they will call me a whiner, so I plod along. The hard part is that one of the garage cameras is aimed to record cars entering the garage and the other is aimed to record cars exiting. Makes sense, except that Florida vehicles only have license plates on the rear of the car, so trying to pick out a late model Lexus from a dark, grainy image is quickly becoming an exercise in futility. The exit camera should be a better help, except that Stephanie Parsons' vehicle does not appear to have exited the parking garage at the Hanging Moss Hotel between 7:30 p.m. Friday and 1 a.m. Saturday morning. Since the hotel services the airport, cars are recorded coming and going at all hours. I guess I had better study the lobby surveillance images.

"Does anyone know Ms. Parsons' room number?" I ask walking into the main portion of the trailer where Josh and Olivia are alternating between starring at the computer screen and scribbling notes on sheets of yellow paper.

"No luck with the garage footage?" Sheriff McCarthy thoughtfully inquires.

"Nope. I think we should tell Richie that his entrance camera only identifies cars with front license plates."

"That's not too useful here in Florida," Corporal Nederfield astutely observes.

"Which is why I need the room number. I don't think I have another week or so to examine each floor's footage."

"Do I denote a whiner among us, Corporal Nederfield?"

"No sir. Simply a poorly paid deputy making an observation with some validity."

"So noted. Thank you Corporal." If I wasn't concerned for my health, I might take a large bucket of ice cold water and pour it over Josh's head. I recall the last time I did that was when he picked up a fumble in the Hillside game during our senior year in high school and rumbled, slowly I might add, into the end zone to give us a well deserved victory.

Sheriff McCarthy picks up his phone and dials. "This is Orange County Sheriff McCarthy. What is Stephanie Parsons' room number? Yes, I called earlier and Mr. Steinmetz provided me with the security coverage, but I thought I might narrow the search to the floor on which she has a room. I thought it was a good idea, too. Room 516. Thank you." He hangs up with a smirk upon his face. "See how easy it is."

"I may rethink about running against you in the next election."

I return to the bedroom, fluff up the pillows and am about to snuggle in for more video watching, when there is a knocking at the trailer door. I glance at my watch. It's only 10:30.

"Shall I get it?" Olivia asks.

"Sure," I respond. I am really curious who could be visiting on Sunday morning. Could it be a damsel in distress or a suspect here to confess? Whoever it is, having Olivia answer the door will have a calming effect unless it is a crazy ex-lover, but since there are none in my immediate past, I decide not to worry.

"Please come in," Corporal Nederfield offers to our heretofore unknown (at least to me) visitor.

"Sheriff McCarthy!" A familiar voice exclaims. "What are you doing here? I wanted to speak with Mr. Ballard about a piece I am doing."

"Bon jour." I think the French greeting will let our visitor catch her breath. "I am Thomas Ballard. At your service. And lest I be accused of having no manners, let me introduce Corporal Olivia Nederfield of the Orange County Sheriff's office.

"I am, like, confused," our guest says.

"I will explain everything, if you answer a few more questions for me and promise not to tell a soul about what we are going to tell you until I personally, or Corporal Nederfield or Special Deputy Ballard gives you the go ahead. Deal?" The Sheriff is trying to do some information horse trading.

"Mr. Ballard . . . "

"Thomas."

"Thomas, I thought you are a sports journalist, not a policeman."

"Things are not always as they seem, except sometimes when they are."

"I'm not following you," our guest responds.

"Don't worry Ms. Lange, most people can't follow Thomas," My *friend*, Sheriff McCarthy says. "We are trying to ascertain the whereabouts of a number of people between a little after 7 p.m. Friday evening and about midnight. I know you were in Mr. Tyler's trailer until about 7:45 interviewing him. That is corroborated by the video I watched. I also know that you were outside the entrance to the concert at about 11 having changed your clothing. First questions: were you there; for whom were you waiting and can anyone corroborate what you are about to say? Let me say that you have been very forth coming so far, but that I will be asking you questions in conjunction with a criminal investigation. You are a potential suspect, but have explained your connection to the incident to my satisfaction. Again, so far. You do not have to answer my questions; you may have an attorney present . . . "

"Sheriff, if you are about to recite a *Miranda* warning, I am aware of my rights and I waive them. And to make this easier, I have a tape recorder in my pocket book into which I will repeat my waiver." Ms. Lange is very sharp; however I am not too keen on her reaching into her purse and possibly removing something deadlier than a tape recorder.

"Ms. Lange?" Olivia begins. "May I retrieve the recorder from your pocket book?"

Emily Lange hands her huge bag over to Olivia without an instant's hesitation. Olivia removes a recorder from the bag and places it on my already cluttered dining room table. The weather lady picks it up and starts recording.

"My name is Emily Patterson Lange and I am waiving my so-called *Miranda* rights in connection with an investigation being conducted by Orange County Sheriff Josh McCarthy, Corporal Olivia Nederfield and Special Deputy Thomas Ballard. Is that sufficient Sheriff?"

"Yes. Thank you." After a three second pause Josh returns to the business at hand. "Ms. Lange I asked you a couple of questions regarding your presence at the entrance to the concert on Friday evening at around 11 pm. Can you tell us in your own words what you were doing there, with whom and why?"

"Sheriff, do you want my reply on tape?"

"That won't be necessary," Josh answers.

"After my visit with Mr. Tyler had ended, and since no further interviews had been scheduled, I decided to send my soundman back to the station with the film we had taken. I thought that I would like to get some candid footage at the concert. To be less conspicuous, I changed into concert-appropriate clothes. My cameraman, Robert, switched from the larger unit to a smaller camera and we went to the concert. However, before we entered the venue, Robert thought he should visit the facilities. No surprise, he had been guzzling Dr. Pepper all day."

What's with all this Dr. Pepper?

"Rather than stand in front of the men's room, which is rather unseemly, I walked about thirty feet away and waited. Robert returned and we went into the concert. We spent almost two hours. The camera has a good sound recording device build into the unit, but we were basically trying to get coverage shots. I could do a voice-over later, if necessary. We left at 11 and repeated the entry process. Robert had to relieve himself before we drove back to the station. We arrived about 11:30, swiped our IDs to get in, signed the after-hours book at the security desk, went up to the editing studio and downloaded the images. Since I had to be on-air at 6 in the morning, I said *good-bye*, signed out and went home. When I arrived, I entered my personal pass code at the front gate, went immediately into my unit, set the alarm clock and fell asleep. I got up at 5 am, dressed, went to the station and was on-air at exactly 6:17 to tell my audience that it was going to be a beautiful day. Any other questions?"

"None from me. Olivia? Thomas?"

"I'm good," I sputter.

"Me, too," Olivia responds.

"Actually I have a quick question. After your interview with Chip Tyler and before you left to go to the station, did you see Chip Tyler again?"

"Actually a little before 10, I saw him at the concert. He started toward me, but was headed off by Donald Bradshaw, the attorney who's on TV all the time. Before you ask, I didn't hear anything that was said. They started walking toward the entrance."

"Again, between the time you left your interview with Chip Tyler and you left for the station, did you see Mr. Tyler the senior?"

"No."

"Bill Clifford?"

"No."

"Stephanie Parsons?"

"Who?"

"I take that as a *no* since you don't even know who she is. Last, but not least, did you see Monica LeMont?"

"Do you mean the woman who was with Chip's father last night?"

"Yes."

"I think so, but I couldn't swear to it. Around 11, as we were leaving, a woman brushed past us. I hadn't met her at that time. When I met her last night, I had a sense of déjà vu, but couldn't get a handle on it. I think it most likely was the woman from the concert."

"Thank you. I have no further questions. You have been very helpful." I look at Josh and then Olivia. They nod.

"Now, your part of our deal Sheriff McCarthy." My estimation of the journalistic ability of Emily Lange has risen-substantially.

CHAPTER THIRTY-FIVE

"Fair enough," our esteemed Sheriff says. "This is for your ears only until one of us gives you the okay. Agreed?"

"Absolutely!"

"Chip Tyler has been murdered."

The weather lady turns as white as a sheet.

"Are you alright?" Olivia asks.

"Just a bit shocked. I guess I had better get used to it if I'm going to be an investigative reporter."

"You never get used to it. Trust me." I try to sound reassuring.

"He's right Ms. Lange. I've been in law enforcement thirty years and you never get used to death. It is an occupational hazard, but that's the best I can say."

"Can I get the who, what, when, where, why and how?" Emily Lange quickly recovers.

"Thomas, please do the honors." I am not sure why the Orange County Sheriff is passing the buck to me.

"The *who* is Chip Tyler, but the *who done it* is still very much up in the air. He was stabbed in the back, in his RV, on Friday night around midnight. The reason you were a suspect, albeit a remote suspect, was because your fingerprints were found in his RV and his cell phone showed a call from you earlier that day. You have more than adequately explained your activities. We have fingerprints from a number of other people who we have identified and some we have not yet ID'd. We have call logs both in and out of his phone, all but three of which we can connect to the people who either made or received the calls. We have toxicology which basically shows that he had a couple glasses of wine earlier in the evening, which we can account for. Cause of death . . . Excessive loss of blood. While there are a lot of folks who didn't think highly of young Tyler, murder takes more than dislike."

"Wow. That certainly put all the cards on the table." I notice that Ms. Lange is leaning against the wall for support. "Who are the current suspects?"

"May I?" Josh asks.

"You're the big guy," I reply.

"We have four potential suspects at this time. Well, maybe another and maybe one less. I am uncomfortable talking to you about them at this juncture."

"But I may be able to help," Emily Lange is almost pleading. "I've been talking to lots of people this weekend and . . . "

"You are nevertheless a reporter." Sheriff McCarthy is trying to ease Ms. Lange into the reality of law enforcement and the press.

"What's Mr. Ballard doing here?" She stammers.

"Simply said, Thomas Ballard is a member of the Sheriff's department. While admittedly he is a journalist, he is an important, official member of the investigation. He also found the body and immediately called our office. He could very well have phoned the news services with a headline making story, but he did not because he recognized the need to carry on this investigation discreetly. He's a cop

AND a journalist and he recognizes that those lines cannot be crossed."

I think Josh just paid me a very high compliment. I nod demurely.

"What I do promise you Ms. Lange is that as soon as there is an arrest, you will be the first member of the press whom we notify. I am sure that Thomas would love the by-line in a breaking news piece, but it doesn't work that way."

I want to get us back on track. "Sheriff, does that mean I will be getting a raise?" Everyone smiles-a little.

"Here's the deal," The weather lady announces. She got real chutzpah. This may backfire.

"What do you have in mind?" There is an inordinate amount of control in Josh's voice.

"You have already asked me about four people, Mr. Tyler, the Chief Steward, the woman named Monica and Stephanie Parsons, who I do not know. I have spoken with the other three and have definite impressions. You wouldn't have asked me about them if they were not persons of interest. I'll tell you everything I know, provide film footage of my interviews, help in any way and I promise not to leak a word to anyone until you say so, and even then, I'll let you see my story in advance for your comments."

Josh peers first at Corporal Nederfield and then at me. We both shrug.

"As long as you don't give Special Deputy Ballard too much credit, since he has agreed not to run against me for Sheriff, you can tag along."

"May I remind you all, that Stephanie Parsons will be here in less than an hour," Olivia announces, just as my phone starts to vibrate.

"Correction. She will be here at 1 o'clock. She is working on some real estate deal and it is taking longer than she thought," I announce. "I have got to finish reviewing the surveillance tapes. You guys get Emily's impression of old man Tyler and Monica. And Bill Clifford. I'm going back to bed."

I glance over my shoulder at the newly about to be minted investigative reporter, who is clearly confused about my *going to bed* remark. I could actually use a little nap.

So many frames of footage are blank. Well not exactly blank, but there is nothing but an empty garage or an empty hallway. I decide to concentrate on the fifth floor hallway. There has got to be a way to improve the clarity of the images. We can find a house from outer space, so why can't we get a clear visual at ten feet? I suspect it is a matter of cost-like everything else.

I am no further along in the process fifteen minutes later. There are a couple of people who could be Stephanie Lange, but there's not enough to bet the farm on-one way or another. Net zero. I cannot substantiate either her presence or absence at her hotel. I better join the rest of the gang.

"How are you doing Sherlock?" I am greeted by the Sheriff's sarcasm even before I get a chance to open Margarite's *care package* to see what we have to keep up our strength.

"Nothing definitive. The images are like all the images you see on TV when the announcer says *if you can identify this person, please call Crime Line . . .* Grainy and out of focus."

"Robert has a program that will significantly improve the quality of the images. I can call him," Emily volunteers.

"Maybe later. I've got an idea." I stand around waiting for someone to react.

"Thomas, we are waiting with bated breath." Olivia starts to drum her fingers on the table.

"Actually, it's Emily's idea."

"Spill it Thomas." The Sheriff seems a bit testy. I wonder if he's eaten anything this morning. *Feed me Seymour.*

"Assuming each door at the Hanging Moss Hotel is unlocked by a magnetic strip card, there might be a record of when the room was accessed. I think we need to bother Richie again."

Josh is already dialing.

CHAPTER THIRTY-SIX

"Can they e-mail me the log for the room?" He gives us a thumbs up. "j.mccarthy@orangesheriff.com. Thanks, Richie." Josh smiles and says, "Pays to know the right people. Someone has got to physically go over to the hotel to retrieve the data, so it'll take a little while to get the information because . . . It's Sunday . . . The day of rest."

I, for one, am like totally starved. It is now 10:52 and it is essential that I provide nourishment to my growling stomach. "Olivia . . . Ms. Lange . . . Big guy, anyone hungry?"

"Please call me Emily," our resident weather lady says.

"I'm Olivia." She extends her hand to Emily.

"And I'm Josh. Big mean Josh, who is going to ask you to leave us after you have had a bite to eat. We need to discuss matters between ourselves. However, if you want to help, see if you can locate Mr. Tyler and the Monica woman."

Monica woman? Oh, well. I grab a few paper plates and start to unpack our doggy bag. Margarite overdid herself. We have several-of everything. She even packed napkins.

"The bagels I brought pale in comparison," Josh says as he puts several pastries on his plate. "But I did get a two gallon box of coffee which should still be warm. Cups, sugar and half and half, too." It is hard to understand Sheriff McCarthy since he has a mouthful of food.

"Emily, there is something that has been bothering me and maybe you can help," I start. "What is Donald Bradshaw a/k/a pink pants, doing here?"

"Don't forget slime green pants," Olivia adds.

"You guys are real cops, not clothes cops." I'm surprised Josh pauses from his feast to add a few choice words of wisdom.

"That is a very good question, the answer to which I have been trying to find out since I saw him on Friday talking to Chip Tyler at the concert. By the way, he was wearing reddish-orange pants. He seems to know a lot of people or at least talked to a lot of people. I am not sure if it's because he is a media grabbing lawyer or is actually a car person, although he was also at the concert both Friday and Saturday. The best I have been able to determine is that he has some kind of business with either Chip Tyler or his father or possibly both. I saw him with each, but never together and Bradshaw always seemed to be huddling with the person to whom he was speaking."

"Huddling?" I ask.

"Yes, like talking real close so no one could hear. When he wasn't schmoozing the crowd or talking with either Tyler, he seemed to walk around aimlessly. He looked at the cars, but not in the same way a real gear head would. Same at the concert, he heard the music, but I don't think he was listening. It seemed that without others around him, he was lost."

"I am going to have to ask you to leave Emily, but I really would like you to surreptitiously find Tyler and the woman and possibly even Bradshaw. You okay with that?"

Now we are talking about *the woman*?

"Can I have my office download and send to me the interview I had with Bradshaw? I want to refine my impressions of him."

"That would be great," The Sheriff replied. "Here's my card with my cell number. Let me know if you locate any or all of the three. Keep in touch."

Emily adds a slash to her coffee cup and leaves.

"If I may offer a suggestion?"

"Since when have you started to ask?" Josh gruffly asks.

"Since I decided not to run against you for Sheriff . . . Again. Seriously, I think Bradshaw is a wild card, but Bill Clifford is on top of the list. There is a pause in the racing schedule until noon and I think we should presently have a chat with him . . . On the record. I want to hear what he says before we meet with Stephanie Parsons."

"Gentlemen, I am still fixated on Mata Hari, who you are now referencing as *the woman*. And I would like to talk to her before we interview either Clifford or Parsons. Now would be great."

"What do you expect to get from her?" I ask.

"Either the truth or a well prepared alibi," she answers.

"Since she is no stranger to the process, I think she'll clam up if she has anything but an iron clad alibi," Sheriff McCarthy observes.

"Do you think that she is secure in her present reincarnation?" I am not sure if she really has distanced herself from her own past.

"Thomas, there is something about her. I think she is an opportunistic and exploitive woman, who prays on the needs or weaknesses of others. Changing her name doesn't change her stripes. I am concerned that we won't get any useful information from her or for that matter get her away from old man Tyler, who will tell her to shut up. If we interrogate her as a potential suspect, we will have to give her a Miranda warning and bingo . . . Nothing. If we interview her like this is a missing person's case, whatever we learn won't be admissible." Corporal Nederfield is clearly not fond of the *Monica woman*.

"I vote we talk to her as concerned members of the law enforcement community regarding the disappearance of Charles William Tyler III. Even if Mr. Tyler the Elder insists on participating, we might get something. We have nothing to lose and we had better make hay while the sun is shining."

"Huh?" Josh doesn't appreciate by literary allusions.

I reach for another pasty. Olivia gives my wrist a slap. "Enough. We can save the rest for later. We don't want to become a statistic for obesity, do we?"

I have just been reprimanded, but somehow I feel good about it. This lady has that special effect on me.

Josh's phone rings. "McCarthy," he answers. Once again without looking at the caller ID. "Let me put you on speaker."

"I found Monica. She is alone and walking along the shopping area outside the concert area. Checking out tee shirts. Should I intercept her?"

"Emily . . . This is Thomas. We don't intercept suspects. We casually run into them." Both Olivia and Josh shake their respective heads. "Seriously, just approach her nonchalantly and tell her you just left us and that we are looking into what happened to Chip and would love to talk with her. She knows we are law enforcement from the event last night. If you can, walk her back here . . . Like now."

"Can do. I should be there in under ten minutes. Over." Emily disconnects.

"We are creating a monster," Josh says and then rolls his eyes.

"Let's clean up since there's no more food until later," I suggest.

"The *no more food* applies to you not to me."

"Wrong . . . Sheriff. You must set a good example for the entire force. Having a gut hang over your belt simply won't do it." Olivia can be tough.

CHAPTER THIRTY-SEVEN

I barely have time to clean up the trailer, throwing most of our paperwork on the bed. Not romantic, but efficient. The sooner this case is over the sooner-what am I saying? Emily knocks on the Airstream door and enters with Monica.

"Good morning," I say. "And welcome. I am Thomas Ballard, Special Orange County Deputy. This is Corporal Olivia Nederfield and this tall, handsome gentleman is Sheriff Josh McCarthy." Olivia and Josh offer to shake the visibly trembling hand of Monica. She responds meekly.

"I presume that Ms. Lange told you that we are now looking into the disappearance of one of the drivers, Chip Tyler, whom I understand you know."

Monica nods.

"I have to go now, but I'll be back in about an hour." My esteem for the weather lady has risen like a barometer. She is a team player.

"Thanks, Emily," Josh says.

"Please be seated," I offer. "I want to say initially that this is a criminal investigation. Not so much because we think you have committed a crime, but because we are required to follow certain procedures. You do not have to talk with us, although I have reason to believe that we are both seeking the same thing . . . The truth about Chip's whereabouts."

"Yes, I agree. I have a bad feeling about Chip's disappearance."

"Are you sure you want to be interviewed without an attorney?"

"I don't need an attorney. I just want to answer your questions."

"Okay, please describe your relationship with . . . Chip? When and where did you meet him? The basic background stuff."

Monica clears her throat. "We met a little over a year ago. I had only recently moved to Palm Beach and obviously wanted to meet someone. A friend of mine suggested that I might want to try an exclusive Palm Beach online dating service. I answered all the questions and posted my profile. Well, I fudged my age a little. I just wasn't interested in stuffy old men looking for 40 something women. May I have a glass of water?"

I start to rise, but Olivia takes over the hostess role. "Please continue."

"Well, I saw Chip's post. He fudged his age, but the other way. He said he was in his late 30's. That worked for me. We met. He was really sweet, but immature."

"How so?" Olivia asks.

"Chip craved attention and demanded respect. His father cast a large shadow and Chip was always blanketed by it. He tried to cultivate the bad boy image. Always accusing people of ignoring him or speaking poorly about him. He was obsessed with what others thought and he had a short fuse. Several times I thought that he was going to get into a fight. He wanted to impress his father so badly, but lacked the intelligence, drive and basic business instinct to do so.

Everything he possessed had come from his father. I'm a good listener. I have had a lot of practice, so I think that Chip liked being with me, but I was getting bored. The difference between our ages began to become a detriment. I had been there done that, and he was just starting out. The racing thing became his life's focus, although he began to demonstrate some real artistic talent."

Corporal Nederfield's phone begins to vibrate across the table. She grabs it before it fall and answers. "Fantastic. How soon? Just show your badge and ID at the registration building and come down to the first crossing road. Take a left and look for a classic Airstream travel trailer and my VW." She ends the call and simply nods at us.

What is the nod supposed to mean? It's for her to know and for us to find out-later.

"Monica, how would you characterize your present relationship with Chip?" I carefully select my words.

"As I said, he is a sweet boy and I wish him only the best, but he has way too much growing up to do for me."

"Is it fair to say that you two are no longer an item?" I know where I am going. I hope the Sheriff and Olivia are along for the ride, metaphorically speaking.

"I told him almost two months ago that it was over between us, except that I would always be someone he could talk to. Needless to say that didn't set well with young Charles Tyler. I guess I can understand because . . . Well . . . I began to date his father. There were some horrific yelling contests between Chip and me and sometimes between Chip and his father. I tried to mediate, but since I was the source of the problem, that didn't work. To say that Chip didn't accept the situation graciously would be a gross understatement. He even started to drive his race car recklessly. Chip's father wanted to bring him into the real estate business, but after his tirades, decided to wait a while. That only got Chip angrier and he blamed me for poisoning his dad against him. He even threatened me."

"How so?" The heretofore silent Orange County Sheriff asks.

"He said he would tell his father about my past."

"Would that be a problem?" Josh probes.

"Maybe, but I don't want to talk about it. I came to the track so that I could finally make it clear to Chip that he was acting like a child and I was not interested in having any part of him."

"When did you last speak with or see Chip?" I ask.

"On Friday we spoke on the phone quite a few times. One call was fairly civil. He basically rambled on about his race car being sabotaged and that there was a conspiracy to make him look bad. I listened, but it seemed like what I call *classic Chip*. You know blaming someone or something else for mistakes you make. That call lasted over a half hour. There were several more short calls on Friday that were not so pleasant where he called me every name in the book . . . And then some I didn't know. He ranted and raved. Once again he said that *he had the goods on me* and that he was going to tell his father. Each time, I hung up after a couple of minutes. I even called him back to settle him down. No luck. Do you have a ladies' room?"

"Let me show you," the *lady of the house* says.

Olivia returns and says, "Tyler's RV was completely wired for security including hidden microphones and two cameras. Everything is either motion or voice activated so that the images will corroborate or refute what we have been told so far or what still may be told."

"Yes!" Josh is clearly excited by this bit of news. It seems like the murder will be available to watch in the privacy of one's own home.

"There is one big drawback. Well, actually two. The data can only be accessed through Tyler's cell phone. It requires user's fingerprint to gain access. Doable, but it requires someone to go to the morgue, which is being done as we speak."

Gross.

"The second problem is that the data is only stored for 24 hours. The good news is that there is back-up app. We will know what progress our people have made when Deputy Gilman arrives. So until then, let's get as much as we can."

"Excuse me," Monica shouts from the bathroom. "How do you flush the toilet?"

In an attempt to sound professional and not convulse in hysteria, I simply say, "Step on the rubber button on the floor next to the toilet." We hear a flush. I glance over at Josh who is wiping a tear from his eye.

CHAPTER THIRTY-EIGHT

Our *guest* returns and announces that she is ready. For what? No comment.

"Monica did you see or speak to Chip after you talked on the phone Friday?" I ask.

"Yes. We got to the track about 5 o'clock. Mr. Tyler had to pick up some paperwork to review before today's meeting of the track's Board of Directors, which should be finishing up pretty soon. I hope we can leave by two and be back in Palm Beach by five. I'm kinda tired of cars."

"Do you happen to know the names of the directors?" Josh wants the answer to the same question I was about to ask.

"I think so. There's Mr. Tyler, of course. He owns the largest interest. And then there's Ken Parsons. He's one of Mr. Tyler's partners. I've got to tell you a funny story. Right after Ken divorced his crazy wife, Stephanie, she started to call Chip. Like, she's a whole lot older than he is. She'd ask him over for dinner. She fancies herself a gourmet chef. Even after he and I started seeing each other, she would call him at all hours of the day and night. I would have been embarrassed, but not Stephanie. Anyway, where was I?"

"You were telling us about the directors." Olivia's voice is intended to calm Monica, who is getting visibly wound up.

"Right. Another director is a doctor. He has a funny name. I think it's Indian or something like that. Then there is Rocco Viscotti. He was the general contractor for the track. Let's see . . . The only other person I can think of is Bill Clifford. He's Mr. Tyler's accountant or something and a big shot in the car racing thing."

You can hear our collective jaws drop. I recover first and say, "Monica can you go back and tell us if you spoke with Chip on Friday after the phone calls?"

"Yes, I actually saw him. Mr. Tyler and I went out for dinner at the Foggy Creek Inn where we are staying. He said he had some calls to make and some documents to review and suggested I go to the concert for a couple of hours. He gave me the keys to his Mercedes and said *that he should be done by 11 and we could go to the cocktail lounge for a night cap.* It was about 8:30 when I got to the track. The inn is only about five minutes away, but I wanted to change and freshen up. Anyway I hung around listening to the music. I grew up on Country and Western. The concert was great. Suddenly, I realized that it was about twenty minutes after 10 and I didn't want to get back too late. I started to leave and then I saw him."

"Who?" All three of us ask simultaneously.

"Chip, of course. He had been talking to a man wearing the ugliest orange pants I had ever seen. They seemed very animated. I couldn't hear what they were saying, but I saw the man throw up his hands and walk away from Chip, who turned toward the exit and . . . Me. I started to move as quickly as I could to get out of there. I think I even bumped into some lady. Chip called after me and I decided to slow down. He caught up and asked me if we could talk. I said that I was in a bit of a hurry, which I probably shouldn't have said because he knew who I was in a hurry to see . . . His father. I grabbed my hand . . . Firmly but not real tight and walked us over to his RV. We went inside. I was nervous. I was worried about being late and I was worried about Chip's state of mind. He was very anxious. Within about a minute he fell completely apart. He was babbling about his car, about how much he missed me . . . Actually he said *talking to me*. Then he started to cry. I hugged him and held him close for a couple of minutes or so. He began to recover his composure, so I gave him a kiss and said *good-night* and drove back to the Inn. I got there about ten after 11, met Mr. Tyler and had a Scotch on the rocks . . . Black Label and listened to a very cool jazz pianist until about 12:30 and then went to our room. Mr. Tyler wanted to get to the track by 10 o'clock sharp so he could watch Chip's practice. He really loved his kid; he just wasn't a very good parent."

"Do you have a cell phone we could call if we have any questions or find Chip?"

"It's 561-411-4151. Please call when you hear anything." Monica turns to go. I shake my head. Josh and Olivia both nod. Now is not the time to get into Monica's former lives.

"May I have a piece of pastry? It looks delicious." Monica looks at the food tray which I had removed from the table, but not completely cleared away. I feel guilty I hadn't offered her any.

"Please, help yourself. Do you need a plate?" I hope I sound gracious.

"A napkin is fine. I'm going to walk over to the track manager's office. That's where the board is meeting. Bye." She turns and leaves.

"I am totally exhausted."

"Unfreakin' believable." The vocabulary of the Orange County Sheriff can be somewhat limited at times.

"Except that it is totally believable and consistent with everything we have heard. Monica's version fits perfectly. She has an alibi which is easily verifiable. Everything she said and how she said it was credible. She also added more than a few morsels of information which may prove invaluable."

I wish Olivia hadn't used the word morsels. I'm getting hungry. Brain cells need to be fed.

"You may each have one little piece of pastry," Olivia announces. She is obviously a psychic.

Josh and I accept with pleasure Olivia's kind invitation and each snatch a delicacy from the platter. "Let me start up the generator so we can heat the coffee in the microwave." This may be a classic, but it isn't without modern conveniences.

While we are being gluttons, the dear Corporal Nederfield retires to the bedroom. Wish I could join her; however she returns before I take my last nibble of a guava Danish. I'll say no more.

"I can't get a handle on Barrister Bradshaw's role. If Monica had said he was on the Board of Directors that might explain his constant presence. But no, she has to tell us that Bill Clifford, who I think is up to his eyeballs in this mess, is a member of the board." I hope I am making sense.

Josh stands and stretches. "I'm going out to get a Dr. Pepper."

"Make sure you have an unwrinkled dollar bill." Poking fun at the Sheriff could be a full time job.

"Better yet, here are four quarters. Put them in slowly." Olivia hands over the change.

"You guys are a real hoot. I'll be right back." As soon as Josh leaves the Airstream, Olivia comes over and gives me a big hug-and an even bigger kiss.

"It's too bad we don't have the security images from Tyler's RV. The case would be over and then the mean old Sheriff might give us some time off."

I begin to melt and it is not because of the outside temperature.

"Okay you two, back to work."

"Don't you ever knock?"

"I'm the Sheriff. I don't have to knock."

"I see you got your drink. Finish up. I think we need to go for a walk." Corporal Nederfield is formulating a plan. I hope she let us in on it.

I glance over at Josh, who in turn looks at me and shrugs.

"Spill the beans, Corporal."

"We might have conclusive evidence if the footage from Tyler's RV is good. We might have exculpatory evidence for one suspect if the room card system shows Stephanie Parson's room was accessed at some time before ten Friday evening, when Emily says she saw Tyler at the concert, and after 6 am on Saturday, by which time Tyler had been dead for several hours. So, we are left with Bill Clifford, possibly Stephanie Parsons and remotely Donald Bradshaw. I think Monica is off the hook and I think Tyler the Elder is off the hook, as well. Agreed?"

"Let's have a sit down with Bill Clifford." I agree with Josh that we should talk to the Chief Steward, but I am not sure the best way to approach him.

"Thomas, time is running out. Stephanie Parsons will be here in an hour and a half. We need to approach Clifford now and in his face." What Olivia says is logical. I am struggling with how to ask the right questions in the right order. Wing it-right? I am going to text him that I want to speak with him as soon as he is out of his meeting. Let him know that we know about the board meeting.

"I'm fine with that," The Orange County chief law enforcement officer says.

"Me, too," His most beautiful, wonderful—stop—assistant adds.

"Done!" I put my phone back in my pocket. "I am going to visit the men's room and stretch my legs. Anyone care to join me?"

"I'll join you in the men's room trip, but I want to make a couple of calls. We do have other cases in the office."

"I'll join you in the stretch your leg trip, but will pass on the men's room part." Olivia certainly knows how to make me smile.

CHAPTER THIRTY-NINE

"We'll have about a half hour of peace and quiet before the noise from the racing and that from concert clash in a decibel debacle."

"Thomas, do you always speak metaphorically?"

"No, sometimes I speak figuratively and metaphorically."

"I guess it is emblematic of the professional journalist but, I like you anyway."

"Golly gee missy. You sure sound pretty when you use them big words." Here comes a punch. Wait! A kiss instead. Much better. I take hold of Olivia's hand and start walking with no particular purpose, except to be next to her. Our reverie is interrupted by my cell phone. Unlike Sheriff McCarthy, I look at the caller ID. "Hey, Bill. You got a few minutes before the race program starts?" I pause. "My trailer in ten minutes. Great."

"Alas, our stroll is curtailed by duty." Corporal Nederfield squeezes my hand and smiles.

"Duty is a cruel mistress," I say for no good reason except that it is the first thing that jumps into my metaphoric mind.

"Better be the only one you have. Let's go." She's always getting in the last word.

We hot foot it back to the trailer. Josh is sitting on the steps of the trailer. "Not comfy enough inside?"

"Huh? No, I was just thinking about something else. We've had sixteen low tech robberies in the county in three weeks and the M.O. is always the same, throw a concrete block through a window, run inside and grab everything you can in two minutes . . . Not a second longer, except that last night an elderly man was seriously hurt when he tried to stop the punks. Now everyone wants to know what the Sheriff's office is going to do about it? *Catch the bastards* is the only thing I can think of, but the quote wouldn't look good on air. I didn't go to the press conference last night because I was trying to catch a murderer. Thomas, you can have my job."

"Buck up buckaroo, Bill Clifford is on his way over. When you announce that you have arrested the murderer of the son of real estate mogul Charles William Tyler, Jr., your praise will be sung from the halls of justice . . . Or whatever."

"Don't worry Sheriff; he's been talking kinda funny all morning. I think he has had too much sugar."

I hang my head. Olivia and Josh chortle. Not a guffaw-not a chuckle, but a chortle.

"Let's get inside and try to look and act professional," I say straight faced-more or less.

We wait less than three minutes before we hear the put-putting sound of Bill Clifford's golf cart. He still drives an old school gas model rather than the new and improved-and very expensive electric version. I anticipate his arrival by opening the door. "Come on in Bill. We've got a lot to go over and I know that you need to get back to officialdom shortly. First let me introduce you to Orange County Sheriff Josh McCarthy whom you met yesterday without his official title and his invaluable assistant Corporal Olivia Nederfield. Let me also say that I am an Orange County Special Deputy."

"Thomas, I don't understand," the Chief Steward sputters.

"Actually Bill, I think you do." I am winging this, but need to shake up a few things first. "We are conducting a murder investigation into the death of Charles William Tyler III."

"Jesus, Mary and Joseph!"

"Mr. Clifford, *You have the right to remain silent. Anything you say can and will be used against you in a court of law. You have the right to an attorney.* Do you understand your rights?" Josh is not wasting any time with niceties.

"I understand . . . All too well." Bill Clifford's voice has not regained any strength.

"Bill, do want to talk to us or do you want an attorney? It is your absolute right." I want to cut to the chase, figuratively speaking, of course.

"I might as well tell you everything. You'll find out anyway. But I want you to understand that I did not kill Chip Tyler."

"Mr. Clifford, may I record this conversation?" Corporal Nederfield already has the device in her hand.

"Yeh . . . Okay. Tell me when I can start talking."

Olivia fixes a tiny microphone onto Clifford's shirt. "Please state your name," She begins.

"William Howard Clifford. That's my legal name."

"Let me do an audio check." Olivia rewinds the recorder and we hear *William Howard Clifford. That's my legal name.* "Sound is fine."

"Thomas, please continue," Sheriff McCarthy says in a, *this is not an option* tone.

"Bill, I am going to ask you some questions, but basically I want you to tell us everything you can about Chip's death. It may be the only time you can explain from your point of view, what happened. Let me tell you what we know. I don't want you to trap yourself, so I am going to start by saying that we have identified your fingerprints in Tyler's RV, which has a very sophisticated security/surveillance system. We are getting both visual and voice recordings as we speak. But we don't have it yet and we don't want the murderer, which you say isn't you, to slip through our fingers. While in time we will be able to ascertain the identity of the assailant, there is a lot of back filling we need to put all the pieces into perspective. Let's start at the beginning by you telling us how you initially met the Tylers, especially Chip."

The Chief Steward glances down at his watch and then begins. "I first met Charles Tyler, the father, about seven years ago when I was performing an IRS tax audit of one of his limited partnerships. His tax preparer was, to say the least, very aggressive and very creative in the preparation of the return. Mr. Tyler came across as someone who did not suffer fools lightly and I think he considered his tax guy a fool for being too aggressive and too creative. He provided me with a list of six other entities in which Tyler was involved for whom this individual had prepared returns and asked me to review them all and said that if I found any problems, he wanted to know immediately. He made it clear that he would pay any taxes due, penalties and interest. At first I hesitated, then agreed. Indeed each return had issues, which I noted in Deficiency Notices. Mr. Tyler paid the tax bills within days. I heard through the grapevine that he terminated the services of the tax firm and reported them to the Regional Field Office. Thomas, I'm a bit thirsty, do you have a Dr. Pepper?"

"I can go out and get one for you, Mr. Clifford," Olivia volunteers.

"No, that's fine. Water?"

"Got that by the gallon." It's hard to sound cheery at a time like this. "Please continue."

"As things turned out, I was about to retire anyway and since everyone thought the idea of auditing the other Tyler businesses was mine, I decided that the time was right to get my gold watch and move on. I left the IRS and started a consulting firm. Mr. Tyler and a number of his entities became our first clients. No one raised an eyebrow since everyone thought I was the whistle blower. Parenthetically, as you know Thomas, I have always been involved with car racing, starting with flagging and communications, moving to tech inspecting and now as Chief Steward. Our consulting practice grew, in large part with referrals from the Tyler organization. I approached Mr. Tyler with a business proposition about five years ago. Let me put this in perspective. Chip was about 26 at the time. He finally finished college after numerous unsuccessful attempts. His father was proud of him for only taking eight years to achieve what most of us did in four years. But price was no object. Anyway, I had this idea for a real estate project. I made it my practice never to become a business partner with any client. It creates an instant conflict of interest. But this was different. I was going to bring a different type of expertise to the project. You see, this track is my brain child. I found the location, negotiated the purchase price, designed the track, got the permits and with Mr. Tyler's help, secured the most important part, the financing. Every penny I had has been invested in this project. It's my baby."

Clifford stops and takes a long drink of water.

"It's a great facility, Bill." What else can I say at this point?

"It's great because everyone likes to come here. We have a car related event here almost every week. That's the bread and butter. And that's what I can do . . . Make sure the cars show up."

"What about Chip in all this?" Josh is trying to control the direction of Bill's monologue.

And that is the $64,000 Question.

CHAPTER FORTY

"Once the track development started to move ahead, Mr. Tyler thought it would be something in which Chip could participate. Needless to say, I was opposed. Not only was he a spoiled brat who tried to push everyone around because he was the son of Charles Tyler, but he didn't know diddly squat about car racing. He thought he was big stuff, talking down to Rocco, the general contractor, and to me. He's lucky Rocco didn't bury him under the straightaway. The kid even tried to change the layout of my track. That was the last straw. Mr. Tyler, Rocco and I had a real heart to heart. Most of the money came from Mr. Tyler and his cronies, but without me and Rocco, the expertise to build and operate the track was gone. We struck a compromise: Chip would stay clear until the facility was completed. In the interim he would learn about car racing from the ground up. Since I didn't think that the punk would stick with the program, I agreed. What I hadn't counted on was his father's participation in young Tyler's training. This is where I found myself being painted into a corner. Mr. Tyler wanted his son to learn about the financial side of the development business. As the financial consultant for the Tyler holdings guess who got stuck with showing Chip the ropes?"

"And you weren't very happy about it, were you?" I ask.

"That's an understatement, Thomas. The project progressed ahead of schedule and we were all pleased, except Chip, who still knew nothing about car racing, which was okay with me since that meant he wasn't going to be in my hair. Little did I expect his father to go to Billy Whistler, who I've known for years, and buy a vintage race car for his kid. His father thought that learning about racing from the bottom up meant getting a small car to race. I panicked. I wracked my brain for the solution to the problem."

"Which was?" Sheriff McCarthy adds his two cents.

"How to get Charles William Tyler III the hell away from my track and my sport altogether. I figured that if he decided he didn't like cars, maybe he'd go off and find some other project to screw up. I came up with an idea. If Tyler had a couple of minor crashes, maybe he'd quit. The kid is driven by a huge ego and I figured he would rather turn in his Nomex, than admit he wasn't good enough to race. I had to make sure that the incidents looked like driver's error and not mechanical failure. Since I often help out at tech inspection, I made sure that I was the one who checked over Chip's car. By loosening the brake booster vacuum hose, a driver would experience very inconsistent pedal pressure and invariably find himself in trouble. It worked like a charm and young Tyler spun his lovely new Alfa a number of times which included several significant off course excursions."

"Couldn't someone find the loose hose and attribute that to causing the accident?" Olivia's training as a mechanic shows.

"But of course . . . Unless the hose is reattached before the mechanic has time to check over the car." Clifford is on a roll.

"How is that possible?" Josh has moved toward the edge of his seat.

"Simple. All cars that go off the track have to be examined immediately after the incident by a race official, fixed if necessary and then re-tech inspected. Since I was the initial inspector, I naturally would be the person to look at the car, whereupon I simply tightened the hose and when Whistler looked at the car, he said the incident was driver's error."

"Jag, too?" I can't decide whether to tell Clifford he is brilliant or he should be drawn and quartered, since he put a lot of other people at risk by his tactics.

"Yup. The kid had more resilience than I ever thought."

"What you have done is a crime, albeit pale in the context of a murder." Sheriff McCarthy is being uncharacteristically calm.

"I know, but I didn't have a choice. The kid is a menace and his father thought he walked on water. Chip Tyler would have destroyed all this." The Chief Steward makes a sweeping gesture with his arm. "But I didn't kill him, nor did I ever intend to hurt him. I just wanted rid of him."

"Tell us about last Friday. Every interaction you had with young Tyler." Olivia is bringing this to the here and now, which is a good thing since Stephanie Parsons is expected in less than an hour.

"May I make a call?" Bill Clifford asks no one in particular. "I need to get someone to deal with the race schedule for a bit."

"Sure," I answer.

He speed dials. "Peter? Bill. Cover the opening ceremonies for me. Stretch them out for a few extra minutes. I'll call back before the first race is gridded. Thanks."

"Focus on Friday," Olivia repeats.

"I saw Chip's Jaguar in the tech line Friday morning with his new mechanic. His lordship couldn't even be bothered to be with his car during inspection. God forbid he might acquire a tiny piece of knowledge. I grabbed a clipboard and asked for the car's log book, which had several notes about off track safaris the car had undertaken. I decided that the brake booster hose was still the easiest way to make the car misbehave and easiest to fix so that the driver bore the blame. Thomas, I want to apologize for getting you in the middle of this mess. I could have given Tyler the heave-ho as you suggested, although none of his mishaps were really his fault. I still had hoped that either he would throw in the towel altogether or that the group who prepared the car would dump him. I wanted him gone . . . But not dead."

"Friday," Corporal Nederfield says once again.

"Oh yes. I once again loosened the hose undetected. Young Tyler entered a corner and found that his brakes had failed once again and spun the car onto the grass, rather forcibly. The car had to be towed on a flatbed into the impound area where I viewed the damage . . . And reconnected the hose. Tyler was hopping mad. I felt bad for his mechanic who was taking the brunt of his anger but . . . " Clifford shrugs.

I am reminded of the character portrayed in Machiavelli's *The Prince*, whose words have been loosely translated into *the end justifies the means*. This is a side of Bill Clifford I never knew and have no interest in knowing.

"Did you talk with Chip Tyler at any time on Friday?" I give Josh credit for trying to get Clifford to focus.

"No. Well, not exactly. He texted me and asked if we could talk. I wasn't sure what he wanted to talk about, but I said we could meet."

"Did you set a time to meet?"

"He wanted to meet at 4 in the afternoon. I texted him that the track would be hot until about 6. He responded that he had plans from 6 to about 8 and we agreed upon 8 at his RV."

"Did you see Chip Tyler any time after the first practice session on Friday and 8 o'clock?"

"No and I didn't see him at 8."

"Didn't you have a meeting scheduled?"

"Yes, but he wasn't there. He left me a note that he really needed to talk with me, but something had come up. Could I come back around 9:30? I really didn't have that much to do, so I went to the concert. I must say that having both events on the same weekend made me more than a little nervous. How would the two groups interact? It was a terrific success. I saw that it was almost time to meet with Chip and started to leave when I saw him and that lawyer, Donald Bradshaw, deep in conversation. My immediate concerns, other than not being seen, were to figure out why Tyler wanted to see me and what was he talking to a lawyer about? I concluded it had nothing to do with his driving, but something to do with his real or imagined role in track management. I waited for almost an hour. My curiosity was piqued. The two parted ways and Tyler started to leave. I followed at a discreet distance. Then I saw him chasing Monica."

"Monica?" Corporal Nederfield is searching for a connection. Josh and I nod our consent.

"Yes . . . Mr. Tyler's lady friend. I guess she had been seeing young Tyler initially, but they parted ways. He wasn't too happy about it from what I could gather. He blamed her for his father not bringing him more into the business. From my point of view, she was good for Mr. Tyler. She had a very calming way about her. He was so much easier to deal with after she came on the scene. Not only regarding the race track, but all his holdings. It was a consultant's dream . . . And this kid was going to ruin everything."

"What then did you do?" This is moving more slowly than I had projected, but so far everything makes sense, although it doesn't really get us closer to the murderer.

"I waited to see what was going to happen."

"And what happened?" Josh is also not amused with the pace of the narrative.

"Well, he caught up with her and they went to his RV. She was in there for about ten minutes or so and then left. I didn't peek in the windows if you were going to ask if I saw anything else and I didn't hear anything. I did see someone else hanging around Tyler's RV, but I didn't get a good look at him."

"Him?" Olivia asks.

"It could have been a *her*. I just didn't think about it. Anyway, after Monica left, I decided I had to visit the men's room which is about fifty feet away. When I finished I decided it was simply too late to deal with Tyler and started walking to my camper. I glanced over at his RV and noticed that the door was open. I specifically remember it was closed after Monica left."

"What time was this?" I am trying to overlap the time lines.

"A little after 11:00."

My phone starts to vibrate. Shit! It's Stephanie Parsons. I stare at my watch not believing that it is already 12:15. She's early. I let out a sigh when I see it's a text saying that she is leaving the hotel and will be at the track in about twenty minutes. Gives us a little wiggle-room.

CHAPTER FOURTY-ONE

If I had a migraine headache before, this is a mega-migraine, accompanied by a touch of nausea. Bill Clifford's description of events dovetails with all the other accounts. For him I guess that's good news, but as they say on TV-*Wait! There's more.*

"Mr. Clifford, please describe in detail everything you did, said or saw after you noticed the door to the RV open." The Sheriff of Orange County wants a clear picture of the subsequent events in which Clifford was a participant.

"I went up to the door and said in a rather loud voice something to the effect, *Chip, it's Bill Clifford. Do you want to talk now?* I thought I heard something from inside, so I shouted again. Nothing. I said to myself, *screw it* and started to walk away. Something was nagging at me, so I went back to the RV and walked in. At the far end of the RV, at the foot of the bed, I saw Tyler with a knife in his back. He was on his knees with his arms and head resting on the edge of the bed. My first impression was that of a young child kneeling to say his or her prayers. I immediately went over to the body. It was warm. Because of his position, I wasn't able to check for life signs, so I picked him up and laid him on the bed as carefully as I could. I didn't find a pulse. It was obvious that he was dead. I stood there for a couple of minutes. I have no memory of what I was thinking. Suddenly, it occurred to me that being in the presence of the dead body of my client's son, with whom I had a rather public ongoing beef, was a bad idea. There was nothing more I could do for Chip. I left the RV. Hip checked the door closed so that I didn't touch the handle and started to walk aimlessly in the general direction of my trailer. Then I saw you pull into the parking area, Thomas. You know the rest."

"Would you mind getting me that Dr. Pepper?" Clifford asks Corporal Nederfield, who, together with both Josh and I, are standing around-speechless.

Quickly recovering, Olivia says, "Sure."

Recovering somewhat less quickly, Sheriff McCarthy says, "Here are four quarters."

Not recovering at all, I don't say anything.

"Just a few more things Mr. Clifford," The Sheriff begins. "You make a compelling case for your exclusion as a suspect, but since we have not yet found the murderer, you remain a person of interest and consequently I am asking you not to leave the track facility until you check in with me. Also, please do not discuss young Tyler's death with anyone. You are free to go and reassume your race duties. If the RV surveillance images verify your narrative, I will have Thomas call you."

"Thank you. I certainly hope this gets wrapped up soon. I've been a wreck since Friday night."

"So do we, Bill." I finally get my voice back. "So do we."

Clifford turns to go and almost runs down Olivia who is returning from getting his Dr. Pepper. "Ooops. Sorry. Thanks." And off he goes.

"He's in a hurry," she says.

"Now that he has *come clean*, he feels invigorated and can be Chief Steward instead of chief suspect," I suggest.

"Okay kids, we've got about fifteen minutes until Stephanie Parsons arrives. We are running out of suspects. Corporal, can you check on the RV security recording?" Sheriff McCarthy has reverted to his formal former self.

"Sir, Deputy Gilman is coming here directly after the data from the RV is put on a disc. He is aware of the time requisite. I would like to get the hotel records also."

"Sorry. I just have a bad feeling that we are looking under the wrong rock. I don't have unwavering confidence in technology replacing good old police work. We have the garage and floor surveillance images and they are basically useless. Who is to say that the images from the RV will be of any real value? Let's prepare for Ms. Parsons."

"May I make another suggestion?" I ask.

"That is a rhetorical question . . . Correct?" Josh is showing the strain of this investigation.

"Good cop . . . Bad cop. Ms. Parsons sees you as a good guy. Try to maintain that character, albeit tough for you to do." I can be mean spirited with the best of them.

"Hold it!" Corporal Nederfield raises her hand. "Stephanie Parsons does not know our identities. She thinks the Boss is a potential customer and chivalrous escort and Thomas is a journalist. I thought we agreed that we can't really use any of her previous statements in a prosecutorial setting."

"Olivia has a point. Why don't we disclose that Chip's . . . Charlie's disappearance is being investigated as a criminal matter? I think we should tell her Josh is the Sheriff, but let me ask questions."

"I don't have any better suggestion, but Thomas, my old friend; we are skating on thin ice."

"Josh . . . Neither of us has ever seen ice except in a tall glass. Olivia on the other hand is probably a world class figure skater."

"Close," she answers without elaboration.

I simply refuse to respond. I know she wants me to ask her to elaborate. "Do we have enough to pull in the worst dressed lawyer for an interview?"

"We know that he had a phone call with Tyler and met with him, both on the day of the murder," Josh replies. "So a chat is clearly warranted. However, he will probably clam up and claim attorney-client privilege, which survives death, although, assuming Tyler's father is the executor of his estate, he might be able to waive any asserted privilege."

"That presupposes for purposes of the here and now that talking to Bradshaw will yield us nothing," Olivia postulates.

"Nothing ventured, nothing gained. Let's call Emily and send her searching for pink pants," I suggest.

"Lime green pants." Corporal Nederfield is big on details.

"Other than Ms. Parsons, who doesn't have a verifiable alibi . . . Yet, and the poorly dressed barrister, who doesn't have an apparent motive, we are left with three phone calls we haven't traced, a couple of fingerprints and a mysterious person lurking near the RV. Not good." Unlike Josh, I embrace technology whenever I can and I hope Deputy Gilman gets here real soon.

There is a knock at the door and I hear Stephanie Parsons saying, "I went down to the timing and scoring building and didn't see you, so I asked a nice man wearing white pants and a white shirt if he knew where you were. He said he had just left you and I could find you here. So here I am."

"Come in Stephanie." Olivia opens the door.

CHAPTER FORTY-TWO

"Wow! Everyone's here," Ms. Parsons squeals with delight.

"I never fully introduced each of us to you yesterday," I begin. "The tall, dark and handsome stranger is Josh McCarthy, Orange County Sheriff. Olivia is a corporal in the Sheriff's department and I am a special deputy."

"We want to ask you some more questions focusing on the time you last spoke to young Tyler around 7:30 Friday night in connection with what is now a criminal investigation. I want to make sure that know you do not have to answer our questions and you are entitled to have a lawyer present." Sheriff McCarthy wants to narrow Stephanie Parsons' interview to a couple of hours.

"Do I need a lawyer?"

Damn, I wish the hotel surveillance was better. I wish we had the log from the hotel room door and I really wish we had the images and voice from the RV. But we don't.

"It depends entirely upon you. Let me say that everything you have said so far is pretty much consistent with what we have otherwise learned . . . So far. We need to fill in a gaping hole from late Friday evening. You may want to consult an attorney after I tell you that we have video from the hotel of every car entering and leaving the garage from Friday afternoon until Saturday morning. We also have video from the hotel of the lobby and each floor, including the fifth floor. The hotel has a log of when room cards are swiped which we are awaiting and Tyler's RV has two surveillance cameras and several microphones. The data is being downloaded to a disc which we will be able to watch." I think I have been accurate in what I am saying to her.

"Then you already know everything or will shortly." Ms. Parsons sounds so calm it is creepy.

"We would rather hear it from you . . . In your own words." I sense Olivia is a little freaked out as well.

"May we tape your statement?" Josh asks.

Stephanie nods.

Olivia sets up the recorder again, but this time doesn't do a sound check. If it was good enough for Bill Clifford, it will be good enough for Stephanie Parsons.

"Ms. Parsons, my name is Josh McCarthy and I am the Sheriff of Orange County. We are conducting a criminal investigation involving Charles William Tyler III and you are a person of interest. I am going to read you something and I want you to think very carefully about what I will ask you. Okay"

"Fine, Sheriff."

"*You have the right to remain silent. Anything you say can and will be used against you in a court of law. You have the right to an attorney.* Do you understand your rights?"

"Yes, I do."

"Do you want an attorney?"

"What's the point?"

"The point is that having an attorney is a very important Constitutional guarantee and protects you from saying something that may later be a problem for you."

"I am already up to my neck in problems, Sheriff. I want to tell you everything. No . . . "

We gasp inaudibly.

"I need to tell you everything and the sooner the better. I waive my right to an attorney."

"Special Deputy Ballard will be asking you a few questions, but mostly we want to hear from you exactly where you were and what you did from 7:30 Friday night until about 2 on Saturday morning. Understood?"

"Yes, I understand." I have to give Stephanie credit. Her façade seems incredibly strong under the circumstances.

"I would like you to tell us what you did after you left Charlie on Friday," I begin.

"I think I mentioned that after I left him, I called and asked him for dinner."

"Yes, you told us."

"Well, I decided to go back to the hotel and change. I was wearing something nice for Charlie and I decided to put on some jeans and a tee shirt and clean up a bit. I was hungry, but didn't want to sit in my room and have room service. That's so depressing. So I went downstairs to the hotel lounge where they have a light menu. I sat at the bar and ordered a veggie quesadilla. I also ordered a Stoli on the rocks. I guess I should have been flattered because on two different occasions guys hit on me. I ordered another Stoli and started to worry about Charlie. He was so bummed out about his car. And I told you about his temper. Anyway I decided to go back and see if I could help him . . . You know cope with his stress and the undercurrent of anger I sensed."

"What time was that?" I want to keep the monologue moving ahead, but I also want to keep our time line accurate.

"I left the bar about 9 and drove directly to the track and arrived about 9:20. I went to Charlie's RV, but he wasn't there. I saw a note on his door asking someone to meet him at 9:30. Well, you can bet I was curious who he was planning to meet. No one showed up and I waited until 10. I decided to go over to the concert. Maybe Charlie was there. I thought I caught a glimpse of him, but lost sight in the crowd. I waited around for about a half hour. I was feeling down. I went to the concession stand and had a beer. I wish I could say it made me up beat, but it didn't. So I had another, which I should not have done. I decided to leave the concert and go back to the hotel and talk to Charlie in the morning. I was beginning to feel sick to the stomach and decided to visit the ladies' room. And that's when it happened." Stephanie is speaking faster and faster and louder and louder.

"What happened, Stephanie?" Corporal Nederfield is trying to make her calm down.

"I was walking back to my car which I had parked next to Charlie's RV. I happened to glance up into a window and saw him and HER! They were hugging and then she kissed him. I was so shocked. I just stood there in the shadows. Then that Monica creature left. I was fit to be tied. On one hand I was furious and on the other hand, I was concerned about Charlie's mental condition. So I decided to pay him a late night visit, aware that it would end well or very badly." Stephanie starts to pace and in my trailer there's not a lot of room. I am not sure what's next.

"I knocked on the door . . . And he answered *Monica?* Well, I just marched into the RV and said *No, it's not Monica, it's me.* He was tongue tied . . . At first and then he said *what the hell do you think you're doing here?* Then I said, *Making sure you were alright, but I shouldn't have concerned myself, it looks like you are doing just fine.* Then he called me *a silly old cow.* Old cow? That bitch is older than I am." Our narrator appears on the verge of both a confession and having a nervous breakdown.

In an effort to minimize the risk of the latter, I ask, "Do you want some water or something?" I hope she doesn't ask for a Dr. Pepper. She shakes her head.

"Then what?" Olivia interjects.

"He turned his back on me, waved his hands in what I took as a dismissive gesture and started to walk back toward the bedroom. I had no choice. I opened up the kitchen drawer were he kept the cutlery and grabbed a knife . . . A large knife and I stabbed the arrogant bastard in the back, turned and left. I drove to the hotel and arrived about 12:30. Showered and went to sleep. I actually slept very soundly." Tears started to form in the corners of her eyes and I think we are about to witness the aforementioned nervous breakdown.

It takes about two minutes before Stephanie Parsons; confessed murderer, begins to sob, slowly and silently at first. Since I don't know what the protocol is regarding booking and jailing a confessed killer, I defer to the Sheriff saying, "Now what?"

CHAPTER FORTY-THREE

Our focus returns when we hear someone knocking on the trailer door. At the same time my phone starts to vibrate. Olivia points to the door and then herself. I nod. Josh is standing next to Stephanie and I answer the phone. "Emily. It's a bit crazy here. What do you have?" I pause. "Well done. I'll call you shortly." I pause again. "Good idea. See you then."

Corporal Nederfield opens the trailer door and Deputy Gilman cautiously enters. I say cautiously because there are already four of us in the Airstream and Deputy Gilman is about the size of a professional football defensive tackle. He dwarfs the Sheriff.

"Got the disc," He says and hands over the jewel case to Olivia.

"Gilman," The Sheriff has reverted to his all business voice. "Do you have an unmarked vehicle?"

"Yes, Sir."

"I want you to take Ms. Parsons to headquarters and book her on the charge of murder. No siren, no perp walk, no comment to anyone. Understood?"

"Yes, Sir."

Turning to Stephanie whose sobs have subsided, Josh says, "I am having Deputy Gilman drive you to our administrative building. You will need to be processed. Do you have a lawyer? I will make sure you are placed in a holding facility and not general population. You will be arraigned tomorrow and a judge will set bail . . . Maybe. I will make sure that the Court knows that even though the charge is serious, the crime was committed in a fit of passion and that you have been cooperative and voluntarily submitted yourself to interrogation. If you give me the keys to your car, I will have a Deputy drive it to our impound area where it will be safe. Do you have any medications that you might need access to in the next 24 hours?"

"Thanks Sheriff, I'll be fine. Here are my keys. Do I have to be handcuffed?"

"It is procedure, but Gilman will make sure that you are cuffed as gently as possible."

"Deputy, please escort Ms. Parsons."

"Please place your hands in front of you," the giant officer says. Stephanie does so and he places a tie wrap around her wrists and guides her out of the trailer.

She stops and turns. "Thank you all for being kind to me. I am not an evil person, but I did something evil."

Poof and she's gone. "I made another executive decision. Emily said she had tracked down Bradshaw and gave me his number if we wanted to talk with him, which I don't think is necessary, but might backfill a little on his call and meeting with the decedent." I guess now that the killer has been apprehended, I can refer to Tyler indifferently.

"I think that I owe Ms. Lange an interview. We can call Bradshaw after she gets her scoop, but before I have a cold beer . . . Or two." The Orange County Sheriff breathes a sigh of relief. If measured by the standard of law enforcement successes, the murderer was arrested within about 36 hours from the commission of the crime-pretty good sleuthing.

I dial Emily and say, "Come on over."

"Let's clean this place up. It looks like a pigsty." Olivia immediately starts to tidy up.

"Anyone want a Dr. Pepper?" My comment gets a raucous response from my colleague, a punch in the arm, followed by a kiss from Olivia and a slap on the back from Josh. I was being serious-not.

Emily arrived with both her camera and sound operators and did a terrific job of interviewing the Sheriff, who gave effusive praise to Corporal Nederfield and passing reference to the help from a local sports journalist. I guess he is worried about my running against him. Off the record, Josh made it clear that he didn't want any leaks until the 6 o'clock evening news. I think he wanted to make sure that Stephanie had been processed before the wannabes hanging around headquarters got wind of her arrest . . . Or the murder for that matter. I think he also wanted the race and concert to conclude before the news broke. He can be almost human sometimes, assuming thoughtfulness is a human characteristic.

With our collective last gasp, we decide to see if Barrister Bradshaw is available for a quick chat. Then decide against it. Once he gets a whiff of what has happened, the lid will be blown sky high . . . And frankly . . . *I don't give a damn* about what Tyler and Bradshaw were talking about. A cold beer is more important.

It's déjà vu all over again. Someone is knocking at the trailer door. It's Stanford.

"Madam Margarite would like to invite you three over to our compound for refreshments."

"Now?"

"Yes. She thought you might all need a respite."

Josh looks at Olivia and me. "Don't ask," We reply in unison.

I turn to Stanford and say, "We'd be delighted. We need about a half hour to freshen up."

"Oh, she asked me to give you these." He hands me a package which I open like a kid at Christmas. Three British Racing Green collared shirts with our respective names embroidered in beige: Olivia, Josh and Thomas. I am speechless, which is probably a very good thing.